OCTOBER '95

by Steven Bailey

OCTOBER '95

For Kerstin,
Carlie,
Angie,
Lori,
and Tyler

OCTOBER '95

OCTOBER BELONGS TO HER

I am not impressed.

It is a two-story house that looks just as uninspired as all the other houses on this street. This one dares to have white vinyl siding instead of blue or green. If the trees were any closer, I think we would all suffocate. Yes, even me. The owners probably paid a lot of money for it, too.

I lived in a fucking castle in Austria. I had a moat. I had tutors. I had my father.

I had Her. She had me.

Once.

I look up at the graying sky. It might rain later. Looking back at the house, I feel that ancient impatience start to gnaw at me again. It is late afternoon. Someone should be home soon.

I have been standing here since morning. No one notices me. Not unless I want them to. It is not hard to hide in the bushes. You would be amazed at how often people pass by and pay no heed to a shadow or a lump of black cloth. It is not likely that they will turn to their significant other and say, "Hey, Jewels! What's that in the bushes?" It is insignificant to them, so they do not question it.

Not until it is too late, of course.

1

That was Hurly-burly's mistake. I felt peckish, you might say. I had been here all day, after all. I had to drink sometime. He saw me, probably thought I was some homeless woman napping in the bushes, and so he did not think anything of it. I followed him to his house and came in through the second-floor window in the back. I found him in his kitchen, flipping through channels on that stupid little moving picture box they call a television.

He tasted just like what too many other Americans taste like. Rotten cow with too much fat and greasy cheese and greasy bread that might as well be shit. Or perhaps it was horse. You would think after all this time, I would be able to tell the difference.

But it has been so long.

I only drank long enough for a quick fix. Now the rest of him is draining out on his kitchen floor. I suspect his dog has found him by now. I suspect his dog has learned the limits of his loyalty and discovered a tasty, new food.

However, I am still thirsty.

I look at this two-story house now, and I have not seen any movement yet. I know the children arrive home after school first. Then the mother. Then the father. Despite my thirst, I can wait. One cannot go on as long as I have and not learn to let go of all urgency when a larger game is in play. Every day is the same: same coldness, same frozen time, same solitude.

I remember the walks I used to take with my father. I remember the lime trees. But I struggle to remember much else.

I remember the schloss in Austria. I remember the nursery.

But I cannot remember Her face anymore. Just that She was there.

I suppose there were times after I woke up in that grave—I say woke up because what the hell else am I going to call it—that I gave into the carnal madness, especially in the beginning. A thirst that never really ceases but is more like having a really dry mouth that is suddenly quenched. It relieves the dryness, and more importantly the Nightmare, but does not cure them completely. You have to keep consuming to get something remotely close to that feeling. Only the dryness never goes away fully. And each day, your mouth is just as dry as before. Rancid, sticky with matted bloodstains, and thirsting for more.

I once went a month without feasting. I knew what I was at that point. I wanted to see what would happen if I did not drink. The desire became more unbearable. After a month you think you reach the threshold of pain: an empty belly tugging on your innards for something to feast on that hurts so badly it cannot possibly hurt any worse. It is akin to having your bottom half ripped away endlessly. But that is when the Nightmare truly takes hold. An unrelenting Nightmare of never being able to die, never being able to satisfy the thirst. And then outlasting all living things, wandering the barren wastelands where nothing lives anymore, and being stuck with that unquenchable thirst and unbearable pain for all eternity. A Nightmare that does not leave when you wake.

The fear drives you mad, and before you know it, you are breaking your fast on a miserable little rabbit that happens to hop across your path. Though somewhat relieved, the Nightmare never fully goes away.

But rabbits have thick skin, a stale kind of blood that dries too quickly, and ticks who have beaten you to some of the goods. It is the same with deer and other woodland mammals. As retaliation (and maybe an exploration of new dietary options), you try the tick. It is small, impossible to chew, and ultimately disgusting to the taste. If you manage to grab one and insert a fang in it to plunder its bloody stores, you find a grotesque mix of sweet and bitter blood jumbled up with its own arachnid bits. It is too small and disgusting to bother with, so inevitably you realize that humans usually offer the best blood.

And over time, you decide that this is your life now, and if indeed you are doomed to outlast all living things one day with that unbearable thirst, you might as well satiate it in the meantime. No sense starving yourself in anticipation of an eternity without blood.

I knew what I was then.

I know what I am now.

But I could only do my best in the beginning. I could lurk like a shadow unseen but felt. I realized I could unnerve my prey with my mere presence, projecting my will to paralyze them with fear. This became useful in finding blood. I do not know how

She did it. She could lurk and work on Her prey for months, as She had on me. She had others to help Her with Her ruses, as I recall. In those days, perhaps She needed the ruses. But I was not nearly as patient back then. I had no helpers. I needed to drink fast.

In my absence, time and weather brought my old home down—my father had moved far away and died by the time I awoke—and as the years went by, a new world transformed before my eyes. Motorized vehicles replaced horses. People flew machines in the skies. And the longer I hunted, the more I learned to adapt.

From the beginning, I realized I needed to stay hidden. I stalked, much as I am now, from a distance. In the process, I learned many things. I learned how those machines called *aeroplanes* (later simply *airplanes*) stayed in the sky. I learned how combustion worked to keep those horseless vehicles moving. I stole into libraries after closing so I would not be bothered, where I poured over thousands and thousands of texts, widening my understanding of the changing world. Time was no longer a shackle, and sleep was merely a means to alleviate the Nightmare, so I consumed knowledge endlessly. If I could understand the world, I might be able to find my way, perhaps better than She had. I just did not have someone to aid me. I was on my own.

I suppose in my early life that I would have known this, but I rediscovered that they had a silly name for my kind. It was a profoundly stupid name. It would have been tantamount to naming the mouse "squeaker" or the snake "slitherer." When I discovered volumes of what people had written about us, I was shocked to learn that I was supposed to lie in a coffin filled with the soil of my home country every night, or else I would turn to dust and die.

I had never heard of such a ritual, nor had I practiced it. Ever since my awakening, I simply crawled up into some dark recess or cavern away from watchful eyes to enjoy the nightly fill of blood in my stomach. Not really sleeping, I suppose, so much as enjoying the blood to keep away the hellish Nightmare. Nothing remotely approaching turning to dust happened to me, but the idea disturbed me. I wondered if maybe I had been doing it wrong. Maybe this unquenchable pain would be cured if I followed this odd ritual. I therefore traveled back to Austria, found my old tomb, and spent a night there with freshly planted soil from the ruins of my old home.

Nothing changed for the better. I awoke just as thirsty as ever, and the Nightmare grew stronger. I therefore tossed the ritual from my mind as easily as I had my own name.

As I crept from that tomb for the final time, I remembered that this was how they found Her when they drove the stake through Her heart, beheaded Her, and burned Her body: in Her coffin. I realized then that our kind was not as immortal as I thought.

Back to my studies, I read what other ideas there were about us. Apparently, we are supposed to be afraid of garlic. Some thought it would ward us off, and others thought it would actually burn us to touch it.

I remember stealing into a farmer's garden not long after that and picking up a stalk of garlic. It felt dirty, grainy, and decidedly squishable. Even after crushing a clove, I barely registered its scent. I dropped it to the ground, feeling perfectly fine.

According to some other arcane charlatan, we are supposed to hide from the sunlight, since it can cause us to disintegrate into dust.

After dropping the garlic, I remember turning towards the farmer's house. The sun was shining brightly, warm on my skin but not really offering warmth. Rather than disintegrating, I walked towards the house.

One delightfully stupid superstition believed that we have to be invited into a house before we can attack our prey.

Seeing no one to greet me, I walked through the farmer's closed door and appeared suddenly before the entire family of four: the farmer, his wife, and their two children. They had been eating their supper together at a small table in their kitchen.

Of course, there is the crucifix. Or holy water. Or rosary beads. All three of which the mother and father held up as their children hid behind them. The father shouting, "Oupire! Oupire!" The mother—who apparently had some holy water on hand—flinging lukewarm water at my face. "We are saved by the Blood! We are saved by the precious Blood!" she shouted in their native tongue, again and again.

They might as well have been holding up

paintbrushes for all the effect the trinkets had. After I grabbed the cross from the father's hand, I jabbed it into his brutish skull. I wanted to make sure he would not go anywhere.

How laughable, the faith in religious trinkets. If Jesus had died nailed to the ground in a meadow instead of on a cross, would they have shoved bushels of grass in my face?

After I slapped the water out of the mother's hand, I grabbed her by the neck. It was the first time I realized how powerful I had truly become. I lifted their mother off the ground by the throat with a single arm.

The children, of course, screamed as I finished off their mother and father. They tried to run and hide, but there was no wall from which I could not simply walk through and corner them again.

"Demon! Demon!" they shouted.

"Tell me, who made the demons?" I said, baring my fangs dripping with their parents' blood. I like to think She would have been proud of me in that moment. Their screams really were getting annoying, and I did not want the neighbors to be alerted.

That was how I learned about the other gift She had given me. When I looked directly into their eyes, I could will them to shut their stupid fucking faces. I was not controlling them so much as speaking directly to their souls that if they did not shut-up, I would tear them limb from limb, and not even God could save them once I was through with them. It was that ability to strike such a paralyzing fear into my victims that got them to freeze, not daring to move. I suppose that was how She had managed to work for as long as She had.

I had already decided that this family was a meal, not companions. Much like with Hurly-burly, I simply wanted a nice, fulfilling drink. I did not want competition. I did not want to create more of my kind, as I had inadvertently done early on without realizing it.

It was nice to be able to choose when I wanted the venom to infect people and when I simply wanted to drain the little bastards. I drank my fill of the two children, sucking from the boy's throat while clutching the girl's neck with my other hand. Children's blood is usually far sweeter, less old and spoiled by years of unhealthy dieting. The meal that day was filling enough that the hunger pains felt nearly gone by nightfall.

Saved by the precious blood indeed.

A noise startles me from my memories in the present. It is a damn squirrel running up a tree. I kneel back down out of sight. I have to be cautious. Yes, I am a powerful goddess whom all these fuckers should bow down to and beg for mercy, but I know I am not immune to a beheading. I am not completely immortal. I suppose if any of the ones I created back when I first awoke had survived, one or two might challenge me and even overpower me, tear me limb from limb.

But for now, I reign supreme. Many of them were killed by the people who discovered their secrets. And

I, not wanting the competition, hunted down the rest. It has been quiet since at least 1952. It has been even longer since I used the venom.

At last.

The little girl is approaching.

I stare as she ambles down the sidewalk with her backpack. She is playing one of those portable video games the children love. It is a marvel she does not walk off the sidewalk into traffic, or at least into a tree. She is so engrossed with it, not looking up. I could snatch her right now, quickly and like a blurry shadow, and only the squirrel could tell the police who took her.

I suppose in a different lifetime, I could have been found just as lost in a book while walking the lime tree path, or traipsing up and down the halls, risking bumping into the furniture or—heaven forbid—the paintings.

I wonder what happened to the paintings. I wonder what happened to the one with Her.

Maybe I will investigate. Maybe after this, I will go back home. See what has become of the lime tree path, of the old moat, of Her cemetery. Perhaps someone made off with the tapestries before the fire burned the schloss down. I cannot always remember things, but I remember the painting with Her in it. If I can find the painting, perhaps I can remember Her face.

Her face—a small reprieve from the Nightmare.

All I remember was that it frightened me, excited me, repulsed me, and drew me in.

She gave me this gift. This curse.

I hate Her and love Her for it.

But they took Her away. They staked Her, they decapitated Her, and they burned Her. If She had been there when I had awoken, perhaps this existence would not have been so lonely, so fucking pointless.

I was staked once. Not long after I killed the farmer and his family, the villagers found me asleep in a nearby cave. Calling me that insipidly childish word and chanting their magical spells while dangling crucifixes over me, they drove a wooden stake through my heart. The stab woke me up from my nightmares.

Unfortunately, they thought the staking was enough. They did not bother to behead me or set me on fire. They left my body to rot while they threw a party in the town square for having vanquished an evil spirit from their midst. They got drunk and thanked their Lord.

No one told them how we heal.

That night, after my wound healed, I ended the entire village. To this day, no one remembers its name or that it even existed.

As time went on, I got better at hiding. There is an advantage to living several lifetimes instead of just one. You get to see how pathetically predictable humans are. There were always superstitions, and wherever I went, the people quickly realized that something—or someone—was killing them off by drinking their blood at night. Occasionally they would find a real one, one of our kind, and chop his head off, stake his heart, shove garlic in his mouth, sprinkle the body with holy water, then finally burn his body while reciting some religious incantation. I think the garlic and holy water rituals were just them covering their bases because it was what their superstitions told them to do, but even so, it reminded me that I could still be destroyed, just like Her. They destroy what they fear.

What they fear . . .

It is a delicious idea.

I have been pondering it for a while.

But the plain fucking truth is that I need Her. She should have been here with me, by my side, ruling this shithole. Two queens upon a bloodied chessboard, toppling kings and pawns underfoot. Damn the rules, this is our game.

They took Her from me before I even knew who She was. Who I was.

What I would become.

What we could have become together!

That is the Nightmare that will not go away, no matter how much I drink. I can become a glutton and drain an entire village in one night, as I did back in the 1890s, but that Nightmare will not go away: the one where I walk the desolate wastelands *alone*.

No life to drink from, and no one to share in my eternal loneliness.

And the knowledge that I cannot remember Her face anymore terrifies me more than any stake or pyre. In some ways, those seem almost welcoming.

But I am tired of being alone.

Over time, my fear and aimlessness turned into anger. Anger at what they took from me. Anger at how complacent they are. They are pretentious little insects who fear dying and do everything they can to delay the inevitable, never realizing the true horror is living forever with an unquenchable pain—a pain not just of thirst but of loneliness and regret.

The millennium is approaching. I have noticed time and again throughout the century how fascinated people become with these doomsday prophets—religious frauds who whip them up into a frenzy thinking the world is about to end. They pop up every now and then. One guy said it was all supposed to end about seven years ago. Some nutcase preacher said it was all supposed to end just last September, but here we are a year later, October 2nd. September came and went, just like Hurly-burly.

I think it is time.

Time to give these fuckers something truly terrifying to worry about. I am going to cure my loneliness. I am going to reign with the ferocity of what should have been ours. I am going to take away from them as they took Her away from me.

And they are going to wish the world had ended instead of the hell I will unleash on them.

It will begin with this family.

The girl has climbed the steps to her front doorway. She has gone inside and closed the door.

I look around. Aside from some light traffic, no one is watching. Not even the squirrel. I move to her door. I can feel my mouth begin to quiver with anticipation. After Hurly-burly, this one will be like a sweet cheesecake to round out an otherwise disgusting meal.

Much like the farmer's house, I do not bother knocking. I walk right through the door.

There she is, standing in the foyer. She is taking off her shoes, tossing them carelessly in the hallway closet. Dropping her backpack against the wall, still transfixed in her game.

Now she sees me. She drops her game—it clatters to the floor, and the *bleeps* and *blips* stop as the batteries break out and roll away—and she wants to scream, but my eyes have already locked onto hers before she can register that some woman has intruded her home. She is frozen in place, her eyes wide with fear.

Blue eyes. A sort of golden curly hair.

I had blue eyes and golden hair once. No longer.

She is wearing blue jeans and a purple shirt with the visage of a horse on it.

"What is your name?" I ask.

"Laura," the girl says, her voice straining to follow my will as it so desperately wants to scream and scream and scream.

"That is a beautiful name," I reply, grabbing her shoulder.

I remember something else now.

I remember what my name was.

When I was younger, I remember eating sweet grapes. My father and I would tour the grapevines every spring, and I was allowed to pick them. I remember popping them in my mouth and squishing them against my teeth with my tongue, feeling the sweet, gooey innards burst suddenly out onto the roof of my mouth.

I suppose the sensation was similar to what I feel now as I sink my fangs into her neck, biting into her windpipe hard enough to crush it and feel the sudden burst of blood squirt directly down my throat. Remembering what a ravenous beast I am, I rip her neck open further and drink my fill, gluttonous and unashamed.

She is paralyzed and silent, of course—after all, she no longer has a functional windpipe.

But it will be alright. She will not need one.

She will fall over as one dead. I usually like to guess which way they will crumple over. Left or right? Or maybe just in a heap.

Feeling satisfied, I withdraw and let go of her shoulder.

She falls to her right.

Blood is rushing out of her neck like a beautiful creek. Already my poison is working its way through her body.

Her family will be here soon. It will be too late by then. I have spent over a hundred years perfecting my venom's potency. She will heal and be back on her feet within an hour. What took me years to earn from my Beloved will only take moments for this child.

I move her corpse to the living room. I set her on the couch. Her family will see the trail of blood and follow it in here. They will cry and scream, and call for help, and rush over to their precious child. They will fall right into my trap.

She will have no real memories at first, of course. The appetite is so persistent at that stage that it will be all she can think of. She will have no concept of controlling her venom. Her family will be her first meal.

And then they will all dine on whoever comes to help them.

And then the help will dine.

And their dinner will dine.

And so on. Forever and ever.

Amen.

Saved by the precious blood indeed.

They will be as ravenous infants at first.

But then . . . ah . . .

Our kingdom will be glorious!

There is much to do. I turn to leave. It has begun.

This October belongs to me.

This one is for you, Darling.

WARNING LIGHTS

Matt Braker didn't smoke, but for the first time since high school, he was considering it. He held the mask against the teenage boy's mouth and squeezed the bag attached to it.

One. Two. Three. Four. Five.

He squeezed again.

The monitor beeped. The pulse was faint but definitely there.

So why no breathing? he thought.

Carlos sat opposite Matt on the other side of the gurney, adding more bandages to the young man's bloody neck. The sirens wailed as James drove, and Matt could see the red ambulance lights bouncing off the street before them through the windshield. He pumped the bag again. The lungs rose and fell as the bag pushed air through them, but the pulse stayed weak.

He tried desperately to get the images of the Knoxton family out of his mind. So long as there was a person to save, processing that horrific scene would have to wait. But he couldn't forget what he'd seen. He didn't think he ever would.

At twenty-eight, Matt was no stranger to blood and bones. A drunk woman who'd lopped her arm off misusing a table saw. A kid who'd had his face torn to shreds by a rottweiler. A mill worker who'd gotten his hair caught up in machinery that ripped the top of his scalp off. Six months ago, he'd been on a call with James to help take a pair of scissors out of a six-year-old who'd swallowed them whole and perforated his trachea. Just last year, he'd been called to the school: two students had gotten into a fight at lunch, and one of them put a plastic fork in the other's left eyeball.

He'd been there at the crime scenes, too. People still moving after a bullet to the head was rare, but he'd seen it. He'd seen the grisly aftermath of stabbings, the unconscious spouse who'd been beaten with a bat, the nighttime jogger barely clinging to life after a hit-and-run by a drunk driver. He'd seen all the especially disturbing stuff they'd never show on the six o'clock or even the eleven o'clock news. Blood and bones was just part of the deal at this point.

The Knoxton place was different. He shuddered to recall what he'd seen inside that house.

One. Two. Three. Four. Five.

He squeezed the bag again. The kid's lungs rose and fell.

The call came in earlier that evening. They'd gone with the police dispatch and been briefed along the way. The neighbor's exact words, according to the investigator at the house, were, "We heard screamin' comin' from the house. Everyone was screamin' for a good two minutes or somethin'. We came out to see what was goin' on because it just wasn't stoppin'. And it wasn't no screamin' like, you know, some little pissant kiddy screamin', like they saw a snake or somethin'. It sounded like someone was gettin' killed. Sounded like all of them were gettin' murdered."

The neighbors went outside and were about to go to the Knoxton's door when the screaming stopped. They waited another moment to see if anything happened. Before they could go through with knocking on the door, the little girl—Laura, about seven or eight, they weren't exactly sure—came running out of the house, her clothes covered in blood, and ran straight across the street behind the houses over that way. Matt knew they dispatched a patrol car to try to find the girl, but he hadn't heard any updates on her whereabouts.

Even before they'd made it to the house, Matt had a sinking feeling. Something about the day just didn't feel right. The closer they got to the house, the more it felt like a deep depression had set in, and he felt an urge to just abandon the job at hand and go home. Normally he would be very focused and fired up to help save a life, but this sudden dread made him feel that something was very wrong about this particular call.

They'd done the usual staging about a block away while the police cleared the scene. They were finally given the A-OK to approach and check to see if anyone was still alive. "Fair warning," the inspector said over the radio. "It's fuckin' nasty, guys. Five bodies, at least two of them minors."

Even before entering the living room, a smell like iron lay heavy on the air, which he knew meant there was a lot of blood. Upon entering the living room,

Matt saw a scene that looked straight out of a 1980's horror movie. All of the family members—sans the missing daughter—were violently splayed in their living room, toppled over furniture and mangled like some Picasso fever dream.

Legs shouldn't bend that way, he'd thought. *Faces shouldn't be frozen in a scream like that.*

The worst part about each of them had been their throats. It was as if someone had ripped their jugulars wide open, continued to rip out the flesh and tissues of their necks, and let their bodies drain. Blood soaked the carpet and furniture. He'd been in situations where he'd had to walk blood-soaked carpets. He was used to the sticky pull on his boots upon crossing a blood-smeared floor. But this had been more like walking through a giant puddle. The blood was so prominent that it had collected and spilled over into the foyer, then the dining room. The iron-like smell was so thick here that he thought he might gag.

The scene was ghastly. The mom, the dad, the toddler, the twelve-year-old sister, and the sixteen-year-old son were all lying there lifelessly in the living room. The toddler lay in the middle of the floor. The daughter lay prone near the living room door but with her head turned at an unnatural angle. The parents were crumpled over the couch, their legs jutting out in awkward directions. The teenage son lay over by the television in a pool of blood.

The forensics guys had already been snapping pictures away for some time when he, Carlos, and James arrived. They immediately inspected each body for signs of life.

The daughter's neck had snapped during the struggle. Her throat was torn to shreds, and she lay in a thick pool of blood. No signs of life.

The toddler had similar neck wounds. He lay motionless on a blood-soaked rug, also no signs of life.

Carlos had to look away for a moment, covering his mouth. James turned to him and said, "You alright, man?"

Carlos shook his head. "I'll be fine. It's just . . . my son. He's practically the same age. This isn't right, man. This isn't right."

The parents had gotten the worst of the violence. It was as if someone had completely ripped the front of their necks clean off but hadn't stopped there. Their chests had been ripped open, and they'd been allowed to bleed out all over the floor that way. Several of their limbs were broken. The father's right calf bone stuck out of the skin, and the mother's right leg was bent backwards at the knee. Neither showed signs of living. No breathing, no pulse, nothing.

Then they came across the sixteen-year-old son. Unlike the others, his neck wounds were fairly simple: two deep punctures, not unlike a snake bite, were visible with streams of blood still slowly oozing from them. When Matt checked him, he was stunned to detect a faint pulse. Even more, when he looked closer, he thought he saw some movement in the kid's fingertips.

"Carlos, we got one!" he said.

He had no clue what happened here. He knew

the situation had prime time, murder mystery episode written all over it. All he knew was this kid was still alive, and they needed to operate on him immediately.

They quickly went to bandage up his throat. Before applying the first bandages, Matt had to do a double-take.

Did I just see that? he wondered.

It appeared as if the puncture holes had somehow begun stitching themselves up. Though the blood wasn't leaking quite so much anymore, it wasn't exactly clotting that he saw. It seemed more like skin had begun reappearing.

The bizarre moment kept replaying in his mind now as the ambulance truck raced to the hospital.

Impossible. Had to be something about the lighting in that room. Had to be, he thought. The teenager's chest rose and fell as the bag pushed air into his lungs, but there was still no independent breathing.

If we can save this kid, he'll be able to tell us what happened, Matt thought. *No unsolved murder. God, do I really want to know what happened in there?*

He couldn't get the images of the children out of his head.

Concentrate. One. Two. Three. Four. Five.

He squeezed the bag.

He couldn't forget the parents splayed like that.

The chest rose.

He would never forget that smell.

The chest fell.

His shoes were still tacky from all the blood.

One. Two. Three. Four. Five.

And those wounds. It wasn't possible. They couldn't have just healed themselves like that. They couldn't have.

As the chest rose and fell again, Matt felt a sudden desire to peel away the bandages. He had to know. He had to see.

The girl.

He wondered if they had found her yet.

One. Two. Three. Four. Five.

"Maybe the girl saw something," Matt said suddenly. He decided not to touch the bandages.

"Huh?" Carlos said.

"The girl who ran away." Matt squeezed the bag again. "She had to have seen something."

"Let's hope they find her, then," Carlos said, looking up out of the windshield. "Alright, we're here. Let's go."

"Alright, guys. We're here!" James called from the driver's seat.

What did this? What'd the girl see?

Through the windshield, Matt saw that they had reached the hospital. The setting sun had turned the sky orange and cast a pinkish-yellow glow on the clouds. Driving through the parking lot, James pulled up to the emergency unloading zone. A nurse and doctor were already outside ready to assist them.

As Carlos and Matt grabbed their gear and got ready to take the youth to the emergency room, Matt stopped dead in his tracks and gave the boy a double-take.

Did he just blink?

Matt's stillness caught Carlos off-guard.

"What's up, chief?"

"Did he just . . . I think he just blinked."

"Oh?" Carlos looked. The young man's face was just as still as ever, eyes closed and mouth open.

"I could've sworn he blinked," Matt said.

"Maybe. Tell the nurse," Carlos said, readying the gurney.

The truck came to a stop. Cool, autumn air greeted them as the nurse opened the backdoors. Matt and Carlos each took a side of the gurney, Matt still operating the BVM, and began to push it out of the truck. As he did so, Matt caught sight of something that made him freeze.

"Christ, Carlos, look at his teeth!"

"Help me lift, dude."

"Huh? Oh, sorry." Matt helped get the gurney out and moved with the doctor and nurse towards the hospital entrance. All the while, Matt's gaze never left the patient's face. Through the transparent mask, Matt saw two unusually long canines protruding from the kid's open mouth, similar to what he expected a viper to have.

As the nurse reached to take over handling the BVM, the patient's hand suddenly flew out and grabbed Matt's face. His grip was uncommonly strong, his hand icy cold, and he began thrashing about on the gurney.

"Whoa! Easy there, bud!" Matt said instinctively. He was glad to see the kid had some life in him, but he jumped back when he saw what was really happening.

The kid's eyes flew open. They glowed a brilliant

pale white, and there was a hint of malice in the boy's glare. His teeth, which had indeed grown beyond any normal human's teeth, were bared like a cobra rearing to attack. Just moments ago, he had seemed so lifeless.

"Restrain him!" the doctor said, holding down his legs. The nurse tried to pin down his upper body, but it didn't make any difference. With swift agility, the young man sat up, ripped the mask off, grabbed the doctor's head, brought it close to his own face, and screamed. It wasn't a human scream. It sounded more like a tiger roaring into a microphone that reverberated throughout the parking lot. Matt covered his ears.

Then the young man reared his head back and darted forward, jamming his inhumanly long fangs deep into the doctor's neck.

The doctor screamed.

"Get him off me! Get him off!"

Matt and the nurse tried to pull him off of the doctor, but the boy was clamped onto his neck tight. The doctor wailed in pain. When the patient let go, he looked directly at Matt. His stare froze Matt in place.

What the hell?!

The boy's eyes burned a glowing white, bloodied fangs protruded from his mouth, and his entire jaw was now coated in the doctor's blood. The young man steadily hissed as his gaze darted between Matt and the nurse. The doctor, his eyes glazing over, limply held a hand up to his neck to stop the bleeding, but it was already spilling everywhere.

"Grab him!" Carlos said, trying to grab the boy

from the other side.

It didn't matter. The patient shoved the doctor off of him, who fell to the pavement with a sickening thud. He then immediately turned to Carlos, leaped up, and clamped onto Carlos's jugular.

"What the fuck!" Carlos screamed.

Then the patient ripped open Carlos's throat. Blood spattered everywhere: on the gurney, on the ground, on Matt, on the patient, on the nurse. The doctor was on the ground, not moving. The nurse screamed and tried to run away, but the patient leaped up off of the gurney and pounced onto him, pinning the nurse to the ground. Matt watched in horror as Carlos—his mentor from his earliest days on the job, occasional bowling buddy, and certified pain-in-the-ass when it came to washing the ambulance trucks—gasped for air, went limp, and collapsed onto the gurney.

The patient let loose another horrific howl. Right before he could jam his teeth into the nurse's chest, Matt snapped into action and tackled the young man off of the nurse.

"Run! Get help!" he screamed as he fell to the ground. His elbows banged into the pavement, sending a wave of pain up his arms, but he didn't care. All he knew was that he had to stop this . . . this . . . thing.

The patient was too fast for him. Even though Matt had him pinned, the young man easily shoved Matt off and leaped up onto him, both of them on the ground now. With lightning-fast agility, he plunged his long fangs into Matt's chest. Matt convulsed as a burst of pain shot through him. It felt like two scalding needles embedded in his chest. The agony increased as the patient dragged his fangs down, tearing Matt's uniform and chest open. Torrents of blood released as his skin ripped. The pain was unbearable, but Matt found himself unable to emit a scream. At first, he thought he felt a tickling sensation, as if the fangs were wriggling around. Horror consumed Matt as he realized that the patient was literally sucking the blood out of him.

A word flashed into his mind, a word he hadn't really thought about since his elementary school days. An image of a creature that ruled the night, a terrifying entity that only existed in children's nightmares.

Vampire.

"Jesus Christ," Matt said simply. The patient let up, screamed again, and jumped up. He then ran blindly towards the parking garage.

That didn't happen. That didn't happen. That didn't happen.

He repeated this to himself over and over. He wasn't ready to go out like this. He was still young. He couldn't be dying.

But he was. He'd never felt pain like this before.

Gotta stop the kid.

With all his remaining strength, Matt propped himself up on one arm. Then another. Blood poured out of him, spattering the pavement.

Gotta . . . stop . . . him.

Wobbling, he stood up and took off for the

parking garage after the kid. His vision grew cloudy, and his mind began to swirl. The pain from the bite burned as he tried in vain to keep blood from spilling out of him. Once he managed clambering past the ticket gate and down the ramp leading into the garage, he saw a door marked B2 at the far end beyond the rows of parked cars.

Run . . . don't walk, he thought, forcing his legs to move faster. The fastest he'd ever run was track back in high school. Those days were long gone.

If that thing gets loose . . . if he gets inside . . .

Matt ignored the pain burning inside his open chest and stumbled forward. He put up a hand in a lousy attempt to cover up his chest wound. Blood fell out anyway.

He spotted the kid wandering up to the door marked B2.

That door led to the rest of the hospital.

Gotta . . . stop . . . him . . .

He forced his legs to move. The lives of everyone in the hospital depended on it. But he was too slow. Without warning, his legs gave out, and Matt collapsed onto the cold garage floor.

Matt was dying. He knew it. There was no avoiding it. Already Matt's body twitched and convulsed. The burning inside him spread. It reached his legs, and now he felt it inside his head like a fire roasting his skull. His eyesight dimmed, and he felt sicker than he'd ever felt in his life. Looking down, he thought it looked like his chest had begun to heal.

That's . . . that's impossible, he thought as his lungs tightened.

Somewhere behind him, back near the outside parking lot, he heard James shouting his name. "Matt! Matt!" But it sounded a million miles away.

Matt looked up and watched helplessly as the Knoxton kid slammed into the door marked B2, pushed it open, and entered the hospital.

"Matt! Matt!" James called.

The door closed, and Matt felt the darkness close around him.

OVERNIGHT

Naomi lay in the hospital bed wondering if she could run around the world fast enough to tap herself on the shoulder. She often resorted to thought experiments when there was nothing better to do. They proved especially useful in passing the time at school, but now she was just trying to fall asleep while the IV worked its magic.

Her mind grasped at images around her as she finally began to doze off.

The nurse filling out paperwork at the counters.

People walking out in the hallway to her left.

Commercial break on the TV.

Setting sun outside the window to her right casting a bright, orange glare on the white wall.

Can't run . . . around the world . . . have to cross oceans . . . times zones . . . ugh . . .

Suddenly, Naomi awoke to wailing alarms.

A dark room greeted her. The night lights above the counters on the other side of the room were off. Even though the window curtains were drawn, she knew it was night outside. Red light poured in through the hallway window to her left. The EXIT sign glowed red. Looking, she saw the hallway's normal lights were out and replaced by emergency red ones. Everything was either black or some hellish shade of red.

How long was I out? Naomi wondered.

A man's scream suddenly punctuated the incessant, keening alarms. It came from somewhere down the hall outside. Just as suddenly, he stopped. It was as if someone had cut him off mid-scream. Once more, the only sounds were the never-ending alarms.

What the hell?

It was the first time she could remember needing to stay overnight at a hospital. She went in for a broken leg once when she was about three years old, but she couldn't remember if that had been an overnight stay or not.

That was fourteen years ago. She was seventeen now and recovering from dehydration. Her parents had gone home for the night. Whatever the nurses had pumping into her right arm through the IV system wasn't quite finished. She felt sore, achy, cramped, and drained all over.

She wiped away the sleepiness from her face, blinked, and tried to adjust her eyes to the dark room. The dim, red lights in the hallway just barely illuminated the counters across from her bed and the waiting chairs underneath the window. The curtains to the hallway window, mercifully, hadn't been fully drawn. If they had, she might not be able to make out a thing in this room.

She reached over and pushed the button on the assistance controller. She waited a few seconds, letting some rest come back to her. The alarm was really loud and annoying now.

Did they lose power? Is there a fire? Lunatic with a gun? Did they just leave me here? Forget about me?

About two minutes passed, but there'd been no response. She pushed the button again.

Still no response.

The hell kind of hospital is this? she thought.

In her half-awake mind, she wondered if this was some kind of nightly drill hospitals did: leave the emergency alarms blaring, turn all the lights off, and pretend they don't have patients needing assistance. She pressed the button again, and again, and again. Nothing.

"This is bullshit," she said. Putting the assistance controller back, she reached for the TV remote on the tray beside her bed. The tray had been pushed away just a bit too far for her reach. The IV in her right forearm pulled a little, immediately pinching and making her wince. She hated needles, and even looking at the IV system made her feel squeamish. Slowly, she reached over as far as she could and grabbed the remote.

She pointed it at the wall-mounted television and clicked the remote several times, but the television didn't turn on. The red light on the remote blinked each time she pressed it, so she knew the batteries were fine.

Power's definitely out.

Setting the remote back on the tray, she called out into the darkness.

"Hello? Is anyone there?"

After a minute of waiting for a response, the only

32

sound she heard was that ear bleed-inducing alarm. It almost sounded like an angry cat that wouldn't stop meowing.

"Anybody there? Hello!" she shouted, her voice cracking from exhaustion. Again, there was no response.

Fuck this, she thought. *I need to see what's going on.*

She stared out the window into the hallway. The door on the other side of the hallway was closed, and its window drapes were drawn. Naomi wondered if there were any patients in there.

She heard another person scream. A woman this time. This one sounded close. Maybe somewhere down the hall? Moments later, she heard what sounded like an explosion. A loud, dull *pop*—she couldn't tell if it had come from beneath the floor or above the ceiling or from somewhere down the hallway—shook the walls and rattled the windows, the vibrations reverberating through her bed. After that, all she heard was the wailing alarm again.

Despite her grogginess, she now realized that something was terribly wrong. She needed to get out.

She looked at the IV running from her arm. The tube ran up to a clear bag hanging from a pole. It looked just over half full. Looking over the side of her bed, she saw that the pole was on wheels. She remembered the nurse saying something about rolling it with her if she needed to use the bathroom. Tossing off the blanket, she shifted over to her right and let her legs dangle over the bed.

I'm tired.

Her stomach felt a little less cramped than before,

33

but the deep ache was still there. Her head throbbed, and this alarm was making damn sure the migraine wouldn't dissipate. While the queasiness from earlier wasn't quite as prominent, it was still there threatening to overwhelm her.

Guess you're coming with me, she thought looking at the IV pole. She considered detaching it but wanted to figure out what was going on first. With her right arm, she grabbed the pole. The tube was securely taped to her arm, and the movement caused the tape to pinch and pull slightly. The needle itself stung as it jabbed awkwardly, causing her to wince. Moving slower, she finally grabbed the pole and let her arm rest at an angle where it no longer hurt.

Drowsily, she scooted off the bed and let her feet touch the floor. Even in her socks, the faux marble floor felt cold and hard. A fleeting thought told her to ditch the hospital gown and put on her regular clothes, but she immediately tossed that idea out of her head. Taking the gown off, finding her regular shirt and jeans, and then putting them on while holding the IV tube in this darkness seemed like too much trouble. She just wanted to get out of there.

She didn't move at first. Her legs were numb and tingly, delivering an almost ticklish sensation up and down her calves. As she let the blood rush down to her legs, she tried moving the IV system to see how much resistance it would give her. It rolled pretty easily in any direction she chose to move it.

Good.

Her mind turned to the screams and explosion

now. If something had exploded, that meant there was a fire. She needed to get out, but she didn't know where the explosion had come from. She knew she was on the fourth floor of the hospital. She could get to the elevators maybe, get to the front desk, and get to the parking lot. She'd worry about contacting her parents after that.

Her legs finally awake enough to move, she turned her body and the IV pole slowly to start walking around the bed. She couldn't remember where she'd put her shoes. It was too dark in here to bother looking for them.

The hallway shone blood-red through the window. Something dark was huddled on the floor down the hall to her right, but she couldn't make out what it was. White lights from either end of the hallway flashed intermittently, briefly adding some clarity to the static, crimson lights.

She opened the door and stepped cautiously out into the hallway. To the left, she saw two double doors shrouded mostly in darkness except for flashes of the white emergency lights. The strobing flashes threatened to make her nauseous if she looked at them too much. Through the double door's windows, she saw nothing but pitch blackness. When the white lights flashed, she briefly saw another hallway that looked empty to her. Then blackness again.

Nobody there.

To her right, she saw the hallway was mostly empty except for that heap on the floor. It looked like a giant, crumpled blanket.

She contemplated where to go. Thinking of the

explosion and the screams, she decided she didn't want to go left. She rolled her IV pole to the right to take a closer look at the crumpled heap on the floor. Her already-aching stomach dropped as she saw an arm with a wristwatch sticking out from underneath it.

"Oh my God, are you okay?" Naomi said, reaching forward. It was only when she grabbed the cloth that she realized this heap was what was left of a nurse's dark-blue uniform. Rolling him over, she stifled a scream as blood spilled from his neck all over the floor, painting the faux marble dark with a sickening metallic smell that almost made her throw up. His face was frozen as if screaming in pain, scratches and slash marks adorning the cheeks and forehead. One of his eyes had even been slashed open, and a gooey, bloody stream had sputtered down his face.

"What the fuck?!" she cried. Looking closer, she realized now that a bloody trail smeared the floor all the way from his body down the hallway. She squinted in the dim light, following the trail of blood with her eyes. It led to another set of double doors at the end of the hallway. Whoever had done this horrible thing, they'd gone through those doors.

Turning back to the opposite double doors with the windows overlooking an empty hallway, she debated what to do.

Is there anyone left?

She opened the door to the patient's room opposite her own.

"Anyone in here?" she whispered, but there was no answer.

Carefully moving her IV pole around the bloody body and into the room, she searched for a light switch. She realized just how badly the alarms were agitating her migraine almost at the same moment she realized how useless a light switch was without any power. Giving up the search, she moved back into the hallway and tried opening another patient door, this one next to her room.

"Is anybody in here?" she asked.

Again, there was no answer.

Suddenly, she heard another scream.

Almost tripping over the IV pole to get back into the hallway, she stopped to listen. It sounded like it came from the double doors to her left. But with these sirens blaring, it could've come from the right.

She steadied herself against the IV pole, readying herself to run. She couldn't stay here. The stench of the body on the floor filled her nose, and she felt that tickling sensation in her throat right before full-blown nausea.

Which way? she thought. *Left? Or right?*

She looked at the light flickering behind the double doors to her left. She didn't know what lay beyond them, but at least there wasn't a trail of blood leading off in that direction. Still, the darkness beyond the windows punctuated by momentary flashes of white lights . . . She didn't like it. Had the screams come from beyond those doors?

She stiffened, alert.

What the hell?

She saw something in the flash of white light through one of the double door windows. It looked like someone had walked by. The lights flashed off, and when they flashed on again, the person was gone. It was just an empty hallway again.

Had she imagined it?

The lights flashed off. Then on.

Something deep within her told her to hide. She moved back into the room she'd just searched and peeked her head around the corner, careful not to expose too much of herself.

Lights flashed off. Then back on. There was nothing to be seen on the other side of the door.

Still, she wanted to make sure the coast was clear.

The lights flashed off. Then back on.

There!

It looked like someone's face peering through the window. Their features were dimmed in the light, but something seemed off about them. Naomi couldn't figure it out. They definitely didn't seem to be in a hurry to escape.

The lights flashed off, then on again.

Off. On. Off. On.

The person seemed to be content to just stand there looking through the window. Had they seen her? She couldn't tell if it was a man or a woman. Their features were too underlit to tell.

Except for the smile.

Why the fuck are they smiling?

The lights flashed off, then on, and the person vanished from view again. It was just an empty hallway once more, then darkness.

Deeply unnerved, Naomi decided she didn't want to go that way. This meant following the bloody trail down to the other exit.

These are some shit options, man.

Gathering her nerve, she began to move towards the exit. She was careful not to step on the smeared blood trail on the floor. Her ears grew numb to the constant wail of the alarm. Despite her exhaustion and achiness, she held her breath as she moved past the foul-smelling body on the floor. The head frozen in anguish watched her like some dead sentinel, warning all who trespass here to turn back.

She'd made it halfway down the hall when she heard the double doors behind her swing open with a light creak in their hinges. Turning around, she saw they were both open, and something was crawling on the floor in her direction. Frightened, she opened the door to the nearest patient's room and ducked in it to hide. She now realized her IV pole didn't make any squeaky noise and was glad for that. She took a quick glance around the room. There didn't appear to be anybody in here either.

Peering around the doorframe back into the hallway, she looked towards the open doors. The thing wasn't exactly crawling so much as it was shuffling in a crouched position. It was definitely a man: he looked like a nurse in the hospital's dark-blue uniform. But when the white lights flashed, she saw that he was smiling and baring teeth. Something dark was dripping from his mouth, and she heard him snarling and hissing. He didn't even seem to be aware of the alarms blaring or the red lights signaling they needed to escape.

She didn't call out to him. *Something's wrong here. He doesn't look right. He looks dangerous. I need to get out. NOW.*

The nurse suddenly cocked his head towards the room where she had stayed. Standing upright, he walked in for a moment, came back out, and then entered a room Naomi hadn't checked.

Move, Naomi. Move!

But she couldn't.

What if he comes out right when I move? What if he sees me? What then?

Something told her she didn't want to find out.

Then came one of the most hideous sounds she'd ever heard. It was a monstrous shriek that sounded like a feral cat screeching through a bullhorn. The walls and windowpanes rattled as the horrible sound assaulted her eardrums. Pain seared behind her eyes as her head throbbed mercilessly.

A woman screamed.

Naomi froze, realizing there was someone in the room she hadn't checked.

And now the woman was in the room with that smiling, hissing nurse.

Is the nurse making that noise?

The sounds of a struggle broke out in the room. Even at this distance, Naomi could hear bedpans and materials being thrown about. Glass shattered, and an IV pole clattered out into the hallway.

"No! Get off me!" the woman screamed, but the nurse continued to snarl and shriek. He sounded more like a ravenous wolf than a human. Naomi's heart leaped into her throat as the woman's screaming turned into what sounded like gagging, as if she were being strangled. Amidst the nurse's hissing and snarling, the woman's gags made Naomi want to throw up.

The alarms continued blaring over the sounds of carnage coming from that room. Naomi felt an impulse to run in and save the woman, but fear kept her rooted in place. She knew she was in no position to be the hero. Her body was still too weak from dehydration, and the nurse could easily overpower her. Whatever was happening in there could happen to her next. A wave of guilt and terror washed over Naomi. She hated herself for choosing to flee and abandon the woman, but she didn't know what else she could realistically do.

Goddamn it!

Fearful of being next, Naomi grabbed her IV pole and moved quickly towards the double doors. Her feet smacked into the blood trail, her socks instantly absorbing some of it. It felt warm and sticky against her feet, but she ignored this. She just wanted to escape those horrible, horrible sounds.

There's nothing I can do, she told herself.

Her heart pounded in her throat. She had a vague thought of the nurse running out into the hall again, seeing her, and chasing after her. That horrible roaring sound still rang within her ears. She had to get out.

She was aware now that underneath the blaring alarm, her IV pole did make the slightest squeak when moving, but it was so quiet in comparison.

The screaming and the gagging stopped abruptly. Naomi froze.

Shit, he heard me!

She continued moving as quickly and quietly as she could. Even though the alarm had reached nauseating levels now, she was painfully aware of that tiny squeak the IV pole made, magnified all the more in the relative silence since the screaming stopped.

She kept moving, taking only quick glances behind her. The nurse was in the room still, out of sight.

On either side of her were other patient rooms, most of which had open doors. There didn't appear to be anyone in them. Even if there were people hiding in the closed ones, she couldn't stop to help them.

She followed the blood trail leading to the double doors. She pushed through the left one, not ready for the loud squeak it made as it opened.

She froze halfway through the door, heedless of whatever may be in the darkness ahead, and spun around.

Apart from the dead nurse lying on the floor, the hallway behind her was still empty.

Not wanting to get caught by the nurse who'd seemingly just murdered a patient, she inched out through the door with her IV pole and slowly closed it behind her. The door let out a quick, rusty squeak, and then was silent.

Peering through the windows, she waited a moment.

It didn't look like the nurse was following. With any luck, he hadn't heard the door squeaking.

Naomi turned to face her new surroundings. There were no flashing lights in this room. In the dim red light, she saw that the trail of blood on the floor swerved left to a door. An exit sign shone above this door which had a stairwell sign on it. The blood led under the door.

Not going that way, she decided.

Moving forward, she saw the elevators. She checked for any signs of life as she went. No one appeared to be here.

Where the fuck is everybody? She reasoned that whatever this was—the screaming, the explosion, the nurse acting strange and attacking hiding patients—everyone else had already escaped. She wondered why no one had come for her.

A thought broke through suddenly: *Even if I get outside, what then?*

Her parents had gone home for the night when they'd left her. She had no real way of getting home. Maybe there was a chance that they'd gotten a phone call about whatever this was and were on their way to come get her, but Naomi doubted it. So far, the hospital seemed completely deserted of any would-be heroes.

Is it happening on every floor? She shuddered upon remembering that she was on the fourth floor and still needed to get down to the first one.

Pushing the thoughts from her mind, Naomi reached the elevators. She knew the power was out, but she had a small hope that they might run on a separate source for emergencies. She pushed the down button. Nothing lit up, and after a painfully long minute in the dark with those ominously red emergency lights, she decided the elevators were not an option.

This left the stairwell.

She quickly looked around the corner, hoping there might be another stairwell she could use. She didn't see one. In the darkness, the area opposite her looked like more patients' rooms and double doors leading to another hallway running parallel to the one she'd just come from.

Working up her nerve, she moved back to the blood-marked stairwell door. Standing at the doorway, she thought the blood trail looked wetter and more pronounced here than in the hallway.

Looks fresh. How am I gonna get this down the stairs? she wondered, now looking at her IV pole.

She heard a door slam from somewhere in the hallway. She quickly opened the stairwell door, not wanting to get caught if the nurse came out. She pulled her IV pole over the threshold, stepped into the darkness of the stairwell, and closed the door behind her.

Here the alarm was somewhat muted. She could still hear it ringing throughout the rest of the building, but there didn't seem to be an actual alarm siren in here. There were still red back-up lights that gave off just enough light to see the steps switchbacking up and down to the other floors, but the muted sound was a welcome reprieve.

Naomi knew she had four floors to descend, and it wouldn't be easy with the IV pole. She looked at where the needle was taped down to her arm. If she was going to potentially run, she decided it was best to ditch the IV. As quickly as she could, she pulled up the tape off of her arm.

Right, so when I get out of here, more water and less soda. Sorry, doc.

Pulling the needle out of her arm, she felt sick as she felt it slide out. When the needle was finally out, she let it dangle from the IV pole as she walked to the steps. Her arm felt tender and sore, and her body ached, so she looked at the steps warily. Grabbing the railing, she took it one step at a time as quickly as she could in case that nurse came in here after her.

Her feet were starting to feel rather cold against the faux marble steps stained with that trail of blood that kept leading down, down, down.

She reached a platform halfway down to the third floor. The stairs downward switched back to the third-floor platform which had a door painted with a giant dark-colored *L3* on it. In this light, it was hard to discern if it was black or dark-blue.

To Naomi's horror, she saw that the bloody trail swooped down to the third-floor platform and ended at another body. She could see the clear outline of a torso wearing what looked like jeans and a dark, long-sleeved shirt. Now that she saw it, she was aware she could hear it, too. In place of the overbearing siren alarms, she could hear a low gurgling sound. As she descended the steps towards the third level, she stopped and looked at it, horrified.

Its legs and hands were twitching rapidly, as if the nerves were firing but couldn't quite reach the brain.

It was a woman, probably mid-forties. Her neck looked like it'd been ripped open, and a single bloody flap of skin lay carelessly open like a loose sheet of paper. Dark, red blood had begun crusting over the flap of skin. Her brows were furrowed as if in unrelenting rage, and her eyes glowed an eerie white.

Naomi could hear clearly now that the woman was breathing short, quick, raspy snarls, like a wolf out of breath.

She knew she couldn't go back. This was the only way down. She had to move past this woman. Taking it slow, she moved down another step. Then another.

It was clear where the blood trail had come from. The woman's neck was torn wide open, and there still seemed to be gushing torrents of blood spilling onto the floor. However, even as Naomi watched, she had to squint.

I didn't just see that. No way.

It looked, against all reason, as if the neck's flap of broken skin folded up and reattached itself, slowing some of the bleeding.

That was when she saw the fangs protruding from the mouth—like two snake fangs—narrow, sharp, and long.

Jesus Christ, it's a fucking vampire!

Naomi had to force herself to walk past, not knowing if the woman would attack her the way the nurse had attacked the patient upstairs. All she knew was that this was the only way forward.

A scream suddenly sounded from beyond the *L3* door, and Naomi knew she had to make a run for it.

As she quickly moved down to the platform, she vaguely realized that the scream hadn't caused any change of movement or breathing in the woman lying there on the cold floor.

Does she even know I'm here? Can she see me?

Three more steps to the platform.

Two more steps.

One more step.

Another scream followed by another unholy shriek from somewhere beyond the L3 door. Her heart pounded in her chest now, her breathing quickening with each passing second.

As she reached the third floor platform, she heard the snarling of the woman intensify. The woman wasn't looking at her, but somehow Naomi could tell the woman was aware of her presence.

She knows I'm here. Fuck!

Naomi didn't stop to wonder why the woman didn't pounce. She took a deep breath and ran past the body to the switchback stairs leading further down. Once she started descending the steps again, she didn't stop to look behind her. She moved as fast as she could, now fully awake and ignoring her headache and cramping body. As she reached the next platform, she turned right again and headed to the platform with a door that read L2.

That was a fucking vampire. A fucking vampire, she kept repeating in her head over and over again. Her mind went back to the nurse crawling and attacking in the hallway upstairs.

Vampires aren't real, she thought as she reached the L2 door, turned right, and continued to descend. She remembered reading *Dracula* back in the ninth grade. She'd been on a monster kick at the time, so she'd decided to read that and *Frankenstein.* Neither one had been particularly scary to her. Maybe it was because she'd seen too many cheesy movies based on both of them, but from what she remembered of *Dracula*, there was none of this hellish shrieking or ripping people apart like a wolf bullshit. Or running through a powerless hospital hellscape.

Is that what happened? Vampires? Where's a crucifix when you need one?

She finally reached the first floor. Beyond that door was the lobby, then the exit. It didn't matter if her parents were still at home. Getting out of the hospital would be victory enough. She just had to get out. She ran down the steps towards L1.

Too fast.

In the dim red light, her left foot missed a step, and she tripped. As she fell backwards—the steps bruising her tailbone and sending a sharp jolt up her aching back—she let out a cry in pain. This was instantly drowned out by a long, horrible howl from somewhere up in the stairwell above her.

She froze. Whatever made that sound was in the stairwell with her. She didn't know if it was the woman or something else, but she knew that her scream had likely gotten their attention.

Get out! Go!

Something shuffled down the stairs towards her, moving quickly.

At that moment she heard two distinct screams, one male and one female, coming from somewhere

48

on the other side of the L1 door. Stricken with panic and out of options, she crawled over to the door, ignoring the pain from falling. Crouching down, she opened the door, crossed over the threshold, and closed it quietly behind her.

She couldn't quite tell, but she was sure that whatever was moving towards her in the stairwell passed the door moments later and continued shuffling down the stairs to the lower levels.

Too close.

Turning around, she saw the front check-in lobby and froze in place. While the alarm sounded loudly again and the room was cloaked in the red emergency lights, enough parking lot lights came in through the glass windows to allow more visibility. Left of her was the closed-off check-in counter. There were smears of blood running all along the side of it. A twitching body was draped on the top of it, but that wasn't the worst of it.

I've fucked up.

All throughout the lobby beyond the check-in desk, twitching bodies lay sprawled on overturned waiting chairs and sofas. The carnage was overwhelming: some bodies were merely lying on the faux marble floor, while others had been torn to shreds with arms, legs, even heads ripped apart. The air was heavy with the sickening, metallic smell of blood. One body lying near the desk had been completely ripped open. The man's face had been slashed through revealing a bloodied skull, his guts and entrails splayed across the floor, and his bloody rib cage partially pulled out and crushed in. There was another man with his head embedded into this rib cage, slurping up the blood like it was a fountain of water. Naomi fought the urge to throw up.

There was a steady pond of blood flooding the lobby. It hadn't quite reached where Naomi was by the stairwell door, but she could see it was slowly flowing towards her.

Then there were all the bodies standing up straight. One looked like a man in gray work pants and a blue-jeans jacket. He wasn't looking at her, but he was angled so she could see that his neck looked like it had been torn apart. Blood was caked on it in a way that suggested he'd received two puncture wounds to his neck.

One of the bodies that had been twitching stood up, her eyes filled with that same snake-like film that the body in the stairwell had. She noticed now that a woman was hiding behind the lobby desk, peering around. Naomi didn't know if this woman was one of these things or if she, too, was trying to escape.

Suddenly the woman made a break for the glass doors. The man in the blue-jeans jacket roared that horrible shriek and grabbed the running woman by the neck. Two more bodies leaped up from behind an overturned sofa and pounced, bringing the woman to the ground. All three immediately started biting into her. The woman's screams made Naomi's heart leap into her throat.

Fuck!

Naomi darted behind the lobby desk, crouching low. More screams erupted from elsewhere on the floor. Further to the left of the desk was a hallway cloaked in darkness and flashing white lights. She could make out more bodies lying in crumpled heaps there. She couldn't tell if they were twitching or not as the white lights gave off a strobing effect here. To her right was another dark hallway with a double door.

She didn't know what to do. The exit was right there just beyond the massacre in the lobby. Freedom lay beyond those doors that were guarded by these violent creatures. She searched desperately for an escape but knew she was hopelessly trapped.

Now she noticed the flashing red and blue police lights outside. Forcing herself to look beyond the grisly scene of the lobby, she could make out police cars lined up with lights flashing. But she couldn't see any officers.

Where the fuck are the cops? What are they waiting for?

Naomi felt something grab her shoulder. She almost screamed as she spun around and came face-to-face with a nurse in dark-blue scrubs staring at her sternly. The nurse immediately held a finger to her mouth, then motioned for Naomi to follow her as she crouched down and slunk away.

Please, God, tell me she has a plan.

A faint hope replaced fear as Naomi crawled quietly after the woman towards an office door behind the desk. The office space was protected by frosted glass walls that would make it harder for them to be spotted.

The nurse, crouching down and holding the glass door open for her, motioned for Naomi to come inside quickly. Naomi ducked inside, keeping an eye out for any of the ravenous people in the lobby behind her. Once they were both inside, the nurse closed the door and motioned for her to follow. It was just as dark and red in here as out in the lobby, and the alarm sounded even louder in here. There were several wraparound desks, but there didn't appear to be any vampires in here. Darting her head every which way, she could see only red and darkness through the frosted windows. Crouching low, she followed the nurse to behind the nearest cubicle desk.

Here, she saw five other people crouched and huddled together, not talking. One was another nurse, a man with curly brown hair who looked to be somewhere in his mid-thirties, and the other four were patients in hospital gowns: one middle-aged man, one middle-aged woman, one elderly woman who looked really sick, and a teenage boy about Naomi's own age. Each looked as if they had seen the Devil and were considering their final prayers. Their eyes were wide and panic-stricken. The two nurses seemed to be leading the pack.

"What's going on?" Naomi said quietly as they all crouched together.

"Don't know," the nurse who'd led her in said. Brushing her black-haired ponytail out of her face, the nurse added, "We heard screams coming from the top floor. Next thing we know, these people are jumping and attacking everyone. We grabbed our patients and came down here, but now we're blocked in."

"We need to get out of here, Beth," the other nurse said, steadying the older woman by placing a hand on her back. The woman looked exhausted and about to collapse. The younger patients kept looking all around in case anything might jump out at them from the shadows.

"I know," the nurse who'd led Naomi inside said, peering around the corner. "I don't think they can see us here. But they're blocking our exit."

"Let's make a run for it," the teenage boy suggested.

"No," Beth said. "They'll see us and attack."

"Some of us might make it out," the boy replied.

"But not all of us," the male nurse said.

"Is there another exit?" Naomi asked.

"There's an exit on the other side of the building," Beth replied. "Jerry, think we could make it?"

The male nurse shook his head. "No way. The hallways are probably crawling with people by now."

"I think they're vampires," Naomi said. No one seemed to hear her, but the teenage boy glanced at her now.

"Maybe he's right," the male patient said. "Maybe we should just make a run for it. Some of us might not make it, but some of us might." The man looked everywhere but at the elderly woman. She looked at him fearfully, not believing what was being suggested.

"Out of the question," Jerry replied. "We're gonna get out of this together. All of us."

"There is another option," Beth said, her voice going quieter.

"What?" Naomi asked.

Beth peered around the corner again, then looked back at them. "We could try the parking garage."

Naomi felt her stomach drop when she saw the look Jerry gave Beth. Judging from his face, Beth had suggested something akin to painting themselves with ram's blood and jumping into a pool of alligators.

Jerry peered around the corner of the desk towards the lobby, then leaned back in to consider the idea.

"I don't like it," Jerry said finally, shaking his head. "If the power's out, then something must have happened down there. There could be more of these things down there, too."

"Maybe, but what else can we do?" Beth said.

Jerry looked at their patients, who were all trembling and hoping the nurses had a plan. Naomi was glad to have some company in this nightmare, but now she realized that they were just as desperately trapped as she was. They had no clue what to do.

Finally, Jerry said, "Alright, we'll try the parking garage. Listen up, everyone. We're gonna head out that door quietly and take the first door to our right." He used his hands to visually direct everyone. "That will lead us to the stairwell."

At this, Naomi tensed up.

No!

"From there, we'll head down to the parking garage. We'll make our way out down there."

Everyone seemed to agree that this was the best course of action, but Naomi shook her head and waved her hands for them to stop. "I just came from the stairwell. I think one of those things is in there," she said.

They all stopped. Jerry looked at Beth, concerned. Beth looked at Naomi. "Was it heading up or down the stairs?" she asked.

Naomi shook her head. "I can't be sure. I think it went down."

Jerry shook his head. "This is bullshit. We can't just stay here."

"Well, no shit, Jerry. We can't endanger everyone either," Beth shot back, frustrated.

"Can't go out the exit, can't go down the stairwell," Jerry said. "Maybe we find something to use as a weapon and fight our way out?"

"If we go down the stairwell," the teenage boy said, "there's always the chance we go unnoticed. Like maybe it went through a different door."

The two nurses looked at each other. Although they weren't saying anything, Naomi could tell they were silently communicating agreement with their eyes.

Jerry held up his hands. "I'm out of any better ideas."

"We'll take it slow," Beth said. "No running unless we have to. We'll move quickly and quietly to the stairwell door. Sound good to everyone?"

Everyone nodded. Naomi didn't. She didn't like the plan at all. She felt that they were trapped on all sides by these ravenous things the hospital's inhabitants had turned into. They couldn't go through the front doors. But she didn't want to risk running into that thing in the stairwell. And she had no clue what lay beyond in the parking garage.

"Alright, stay close to me," Beth told everyone, crawling to the front of the group. "Keep low and move quietly. We're just taking a right to the stairwell door."

Crouching low, Beth moved back to the office door. Opening it slowly and quietly, she peered outside. After a moment, she waved for everyone else to move forward. Jerry went first through the door, leading the rest of them. Naomi, who followed last, thought they all looked like cattle going to the slaughterhouse in this light. Once Naomi crept through the threshold, Beth closed the glass door behind her and took up the rear of the group.

The alarms were unbearably loud now. The red and flashing white lights were disorienting, and the stench made her feel nauseous again. Naomi could see that Jerry had reached the stairwell door and was holding it open for everyone. The patients moved quickly and quietly towards the door. As she moved past the front desk, she glanced briefly at the lobby. Two people were still ripping their victim to shreds, while another stood staring out the glass doors. Several more seemed to be finally waking up, sitting with that awful white glow in their eyes, fangs bared. There was no doubt these were vampires.

None of them seemed to notice the patients sneaking through the stairwell door behind them.

Naomi froze. The other patients did as well. They'd all felt it.

Sensed it.

A sudden fear like she'd never known before in her life seized Naomi. She quickly turned her head towards the glass doors. Something was out there in the parking lot. Something amongst the flashing police cars. She didn't know what it was, but she could sense it. They all could. It was something sinister. Something burning with anger.

Even though she couldn't see whatever it was, she felt its presence. The screaming alarm seemed more welcoming in contrast to this feeling. Whatever it was, she wanted as far away from that lobby as possible. She knew it was right outside in the parking lot somewhere.

Someone touched her shoulder.

Startled, she turned and saw Beth motioning for her to hurry up. In her fear, she'd stopped moving. Beth wanted to escape that dreadful feeling just as much as she did. Naomi quickly moved into the stairwell with Beth right behind her.

Jerry closed the door behind them. Once more in the dimly lit stairwell, the alarm screams were dulled. Everyone gathered on the platform. Jerry turned to face them all.

"Alright," he whispered to everyone, holding a finger to his lips. "Quickly and quietly, follow me."

They moved down the stairs to the lower level in a single-file march behind Jerry. The younger woman helped the older woman walk down the steps. Naomi rubbed her arm where the IV needle had been. The spot felt sore and itchy.

No one said anything as they marched to the

lower level, and then to the next. They passed a door marked B1. It looked pitched black inside. Naomi shuddered, worried that something might jump out and attack them as they passed it.

Even though they'd left that dreadful sensation behind in the lobby above them, Naomi was no less on edge. Somehow the quietness of the stairwell unnerved her. She remembered that howl from when she was in here before, and now she had no clue if the vampire was above them or waiting for them below.

She had no idea where it was.

As they moved further down, the screams of the alarms got quieter and quieter. The red lights still shone the way, but increasingly the only sound she could hear was the shuffling of their own feet down the stairwell. They reached the bottom landing which was two floors directly below the lobby where they'd come from. Before them was a door marked B2. They gathered around it. Naomi saw Jerry looking through the dark window. All she could make out was pitch blackness beyond.

"Okay," Jerry said. "Everybody here?"

"Everyone's here," Beth replied.

Jerry looked through the window again. "Okay. Looks like there's no power in the garage at all. There is an alarm light stationed above the door though. It's gonna be mostly dark out there, but we'll have a little light."

"Jesus Christ," the male patient said, a note of panic in his voice.

"Alright, look," Beth said to them. "The entrance

ramp is a straight shot forward to the other side of the garage. We'll just walk straight from the stairs towards it 'til we get there. From there, we can get out. Get to a phone, call the police. Whatever, we'll be home free."

"It's pitch black out there!" the man said a little louder now. "We don't know what's out there!"

Jerry held up a hand. "Let's not lose it just yet. We'll stick together, alright? I'll lead. Everyone, line up. Put a hand on the shoulder in front of you. Beth, will you take the rear?"

"Yes," Beth said, coming behind Naomi. The rest anxiously lined up. Jerry led in front, followed by the man, then the woman, then the elderly woman, and then the teenage boy. As Naomi lined up behind the boy and put her left hand on his shoulder, she felt a sudden urge to break free from this group and try something—literally anything—else.

It felt as if she were joining a death march. She would rather leap from a window or run headfirst through the lobby even. Everything in her body told her not to go into that parking garage. Jerry opened the door with a squeak, then motioned for them to follow quietly into the darkness.

The line moved slowly into the parking garage. The single white light above the stairs wasn't flashing on and off here, so it gave off enough illumination for them to see the three steps descending to the garage floor. Once they reached the bottom of the steps, though, they were in near total darkness.

Naomi thought she could see moonlight shining

on the entrance ramp on the far side of the garage, but the entrance looked like it curved upward, and so there was very little visibility.

She didn't know how the hospital's electricity was set up. She wondered why there wasn't a backup generator or something.

Maybe there is, and something happened to that, too.

Shuddering at the thought, she kept her hand on the boy's shoulder in front of her. She heard Beth quietly close the door behind them, then felt Beth put her hand on her shoulder.

The group marched silently forward into the dark parking garage. Within a few moments, they were surrounded by near total blackness. The white light above the stairs just barely reflected off of the windshields of the cars parked on either side of them. Otherwise, she couldn't even see the boy in front of her. She couldn't even see her own left hand resting on his shoulder.

Out here, it was quiet. Too quiet. The further they walked in, the more distant the alarm grew. Soon, the patter of their shuffling feet was the predominant sound. Distantly she could hear the outside traffic and wind, but the darkness was so oppressive that even those sounds seemed unusually muted. It was like a darkness that could be felt. That horrified feeling they'd gotten in the lobby hadn't fully left, and now it seemed to be getting stronger again.

The smell didn't help. For the most part, the garage smelled of cars, oil, and maybe a hint of pot. But there was no mistaking that sickly bitter smell of blood which Naomi had become far too familiar with that night. And it wasn't in just one location to their left but also to their right. No one wanted to say it, but she sensed they were all thinking the same thing.

There are dead bodies here.

Something to their right skittered in the darkness. They all stopped to listen. Naomi wanted to believe she'd just heard a rat or a squirrel, some benign creature that might easily have wandered in from outside the garage. After another moment of silence, they continued into the darkness.

Naomi tried to push the oppressive feeling out. There weren't bodies all around them. There weren't deranged people lurking in the darkness. This was just an unpleasant nightmare from which she'd soon wake up. Come Wednesday, she'd be back in Mrs. Friston's British Lit class and taking her makeup quiz on *The Wife of Bath's Tale*. Naomi tried to picture something pleasant in her mind. She thought of those brightly colored binders the younger girls all had, with the neon colors and the animals.

Anything to distract from what may be lurking in the dark here.

She began to imagine those brightly colored animals coming to life and leaping off the binder before hiding in the dark places of this garage, waiting to pounce. Soon her imagination gave way to images of sharp-fanged creatures leaping out at her, and she ended up even more unnerved. Shuddering, she just kept marching with the others.

Not too much further. You can do this.

They were now about halfway through the

garage. The floor gradually dipped down and leveled out somewhat. The entrance ramp was now angled so that she could see some more of the parking lot lights seeping in. She was glad to see some more light, but the darkness around them felt like it was growing thicker somehow.

Something skittered to her left, and they all froze again. They waited, hearts pounding, breaths held. They didn't hear it again after a few moments, so they continued. Almost as soon as they started walking again, she heard shuffling to her right. Then some movement to her left.

Up ahead, she dimly heard Jerry whisper, "Hold up." They all stopped moving again, and so did the skittering and shuffling. She felt the boy in front of her tense up. He seemed to be getting ready to make a run for it. After a moment, they continued walking.

The noises on either side began again as well. They stopped once more, and so did the noises. When they stopped, her foot landed on something sticky and warm. Up until now, the garage floor had been really cold through her socks. But when she pulled her foot up, the warm, sticky matting pulled on the fabrics of her sock. Putting her foot back down, it landed in more of the same, warm substance.

I'm standing in blood.

She tried to push the teenager ahead of her slightly to urge him to move, but he didn't budge. None of them did.

The hell are we waiting for?!

She held her breath. Her heart beat faster now. Why weren't they moving? She wanted to get out of there as fast as possible. She felt a sudden impulse to run blindly into the darkness. Whatever was in there with them, it had a malicious intent. She could feel it.

Then she saw the eyes.

They were the same eyes she'd seen on the person in the stairwell, glowing white like cat eyes in the dark. They stared at the group from her left.

She wanted to scream out, wanted to alert them to the danger. But there was a part of her that didn't want to believe this horror was her reality. Maybe her eyes hadn't fully adjusted to the darkness yet, so maybe this was all her imagination.

But when she closed her eyes and opened them again, there were now four sets of eyes looking at them. Five sets. Six sets.

More skittering to her right.

She turned and saw eyes glaring back at them from the darkness. There were eyes and quiet shuffling on all sides of them now.

She heard the boy's breathing quicken.

They see them too, she thought.

She heard someone whisper something up front. She was worried the talking was too loud, especially now since it was the only sound she really heard aside from the shuffling figures in the dark around them. Her socks were thoroughly soaked, and her feet felt coated with blood.

The teenage boy suddenly whispered to her, "Get ready to run. Pass it along."

Naomi turned her head towards Beth. "Get ready to run."

"Okay," Beth whispered back as lightly as possible. Naomi detected the terror in Beth's voice, that little intonation that said she had no faith in that idea.

After all the sneaking around and hiding she'd done tonight, Naomi knew the final moments of do-or-die were upon her. They were going to run. Some of them, if not all of them, would not escape.

She realized that although she heard shuffling still, the eyes on either side weren't really moving. She'd even begun to hear slight snarling, much like the person in the stairwell had snarled. But the eyes weren't moving at all. They just stared and held the small group in their gaze.

"Oh shit," the teenage boy said.

"Shh!" someone up ahead said.

"They're on the fucking ceiling!" he shouted.

Naomi looked up. Terror gripped her as she saw eyes staring back at them from above. These eyes moved in circles, never looking away from them. It was as if the creatures were waiting for them to make a move.

They can climb on the ceiling, she thought in horror.

Suddenly Beth's hand let go of her shoulder, and Beth let out a horrific scream.

Whirling around, Naomi saw Beth being dragged off by a much larger shape into the darkness of the garage. Beth's screams were now coming from somewhere amongst the parked cars.

"Shit! Run!" the teenage boy shouted, fleeing suddenly.

"JP, wait!" Jerry shouted, but it was too late. Everyone broke into a run. Naomi bolted headfirst towards the entrance ramp. Beth's screams grew quieter the further they ran. Naomi vaguely registered Beth's screaming turning into what sounded like being strangled, and then suddenly going silent.

The creatures shrieked all at once, blasting Naomi's eardrums with that terrifying howl. The unnerving wailing came from all sides of her now, an unholy chorus of roaring and screaming and snarling. The patients ahead of her screamed in panic. Somewhere in the mix of unearthly howling and screaming patients and shuffling feet, she heard Jerry shout, "Go! Go! Go! Go! Go!"

Then she heard the teenage boy screaming somewhere to her left. It sounded as if he were being dragged away as Beth had been.

Then she heard one of the women scream somewhere to her right.

There was a scuffle up ahead in the darkness. She could just make out the dark shape of something leaping onto what she thought was Jerry before both tumbled out of view into the darkness.

"Fuck!" Jerry shouted. It was the last thing he ever shouted.

Naomi didn't even register the screams of the other man or the older woman as they seemed to be coming from the ceiling now. All she focused on was running forward. She ignored the coldness of the garage floor, ignored the sticky patter her blood-soaked socks made as they smacked the pavement.

She just had to get out.

She tripped on something heavy. Tumbling headfirst, she landed on her hands and arms. Even in the darkness, she could tell she'd tripped over a body. It wasn't moving. She was now seated in a pool of its blood. And its eyes were starting to glow white.

She screamed. The snarls, howls, and screams were all around her. She got back up on her feet and ran faster than she'd ever run in her life. Her eyes were set on the entrance ramp before her. The smell of death was all around.

She didn't think about it. She just kept running.

The light from beyond the entrance ramp grew stronger as she got nearer. She saw more bodies lying around now, some torn to pieces, some still being sucked on by vampires.

She couldn't focus on them now. She had to get out. If she stopped to dwell on the carnage around her, she would die. If she stopped to help any of the people she'd just escaped with, she would die. This was a place of death, and she needed to get out.

Go! Go! Go!

It was so close now.

Ten feet.

Five feet.

Another unholy chorus of that inhuman howling from the depths of the garage behind her.

She reached the entrance ramp.

She leaped over the ticket gate and almost tripped again, but she maintained her footing. The screaming continued behind her as she realized she was finally out of the parking garage. The cool, October air felt like heaven against her skin in contrast to the stuffy garage of death. The night sky was dark-purple. The stars were out. Parking lot lamps shone in all their infinite glory.

Naomi didn't stop running to see if anything followed her. She didn't stop running to see who of her companions had made it out. Turning left towards the parking lot, she ran around the front end of the hospital. Remembering that she was now in full view of the lobby, she ducked low behind some shrubbery as she made her way towards the parking lot facing the hospital. She passed an overturned gurney covered in blood next to an empty ambulance vehicle. The police cars situated just outside the lobby doors all flashed their red and blue lights. She could now see that some of them had doors open. There looked to be at least four of them here.

Naomi ran towards the police cars and turned her head towards the hospital. She was alarmed to see how much it looked like an abandoned war zone from here. Aside from the glow of red lights on virtually every floor, the place looked completely blacked out. In a few places the windows had even been shattered. Up on the third floor, there appeared to be an orange glow spreading. Black smoke billowed out of the shattered windows. The alarms could be dimly heard from out here.

Finally, she stopped to catch her breath against the nearest police car's hood. She spun around to see if anything had followed her out of the parking garage. There was nothing behind her. Crouching low, she moved toward the car's open door.

Hope the cops know what's going on, she thought.

Once she was behind the open police car door, she was disappointed to see nobody there.

Where's the officer?

She peered out from behind the car door at the lobby. She could just make out the shadowy shapes of the people inside, walking around aimlessly. They didn't seem to know she was out there watching them.

Why could she not shake the feeling that she was still being watched? It felt like eyes boring into the back of her skull, but it also felt like a dark shroud was slowly enveloping her very soul, telling her that there was no hope, and death would come soon and violently.

She looked around but didn't see anyone.

And then it hit her: there was *nobody* around. No police. No bystanders. No hospital staff.

No one.

She was completely alone.

Where is everyone?

She crawled around the back of the police car to see if anyone was hiding.

Maybe they came and saw those things. Maybe they're hiding to figure out how to stop them.

When she came around the police car, a lump caught in her throat.

Three police officers were lying in a pool of their own blood on the ground, all men. Each was lying face up, staring at the sky. Their necks looked as if they had been torn open by some animal. Blood had soaked their already dark uniforms. Their guns lay carelessly on the ground next to them, drawn but no longer at the ready.

Their eyes were the worst part of it. Each of them had that horrible white glow.

And their bodies were starting to twitch.

Naomi realized that the officers had been attacked. Maybe they'd called for backup before it was too late, maybe not.

It then dawned on her that no one else had made it out of the garage.

She knew she wasn't safe here. She had to get out of here. Out of this parking lot. And if they were out there in the streets already, then the streets weren't safe. She needed to get home, get her parents, and get the hell out of there.

She tiptoed over to the nearest officer and grabbed his gun. She didn't know how many bullets it carried, but she felt it was better to carry this than go empty-handed. Before she could run, something made her freeze in place. All the will to run left her and had been replaced with the dread that it was already too late to escape her death.

She turned and looked towards the lobby.

A woman cloaked in an unusual garb stood there. She wore a black gown with long, shredded black sleeves. The hood of her garment was thrown back to reveal long, dark hair. The woman stared at the lobby doors, hands by her side.

Move your ass, Naomi. Run. Run. RUN!

She didn't know who this woman was. She didn't know what part she'd played in tonight's horror show.

All she knew was that this woman was dangerous. She could feel the bloodlust pulsating from her like a tremor to the soul. Naomi willed herself to move, but her body would not listen.

Suddenly, the woman turned around and stared at Naomi. Her face was pale and read of anger mixed with sudden surprise.

The woman smiled as if satisfied to see her there.

Naomi felt whatever courage she had piss out of her. She knew she could jump in the police car, which still had its key in the ignition, and take off. She could probably use the radio to call for help. But the aura of fear this woman in black emitted was too great. She couldn't move. Couldn't even blink.

She felt that if she moved, this woman would pounce faster than the speed of light and tear her to pieces. Death almost seemed like a welcome alternative to the fear that seized her now.

The woman approached her, walking patiently as if out for a casual nighttime stroll in a hospital parking lot. Naomi found herself wishing the woman would just kill her and get it over with. The delay was the worst part.

She stopped in front of Naomi and put her hand on Naomi's shoulder. The touch felt icy cold, and her shoulder muscles tensed up. "I must say," the woman said in a darkly warm and silvery voice, "I am amazed you made it outside alive."

Naomi could see the tips of two fangs poking out from under her top lip as the woman grinned at her. Naomi couldn't move, couldn't speak. She felt a tear roll down her eye.

The woman looked up at the sky. "It is a beautiful night. The stars are all out. The moon glows modestly, giving us a peek at only half of its magnificence. And everywhere I look, death is in the air. You can just . . . taste it." The woman licked her lips and grinned. Her vampiric fangs bared, the woman's smile looked unsettlingly unhinged and calm at the same time.

Naomi had spent many days in boring classes distracting herself with thought experiments. *If I could eat myself starting with my toes, could I literally eat myself out of existence? If our circumstances determine our outcome, then do we have free will or are our choices predetermined for us?* And of course, the all-time classic: *If I had to die, how would I want to go out?*

She'd thought about the usual ways like drowning, getting shot, airplane crash, eaten by a lion, homicidal clown with a knife. She'd never imagined it would come at the hands of a vampire. Until tonight, vampires were something out of really old, boring books. Until tonight, vampires weren't real.

But this woman was very real.

The woman now looked straight into Naomi's eyes, and she knew this was it. Her moment to die had come at last. In spite of all she'd been through tonight, it was going to end here. None of it mattered. She should have just given up in the parking garage when she had a chance. At least then, she wouldn't have seen what killed her. But now, looking into this woman's horrible, awful eyes whose beauty belied a malice that seemed too ancient to cure, Naomi let loose more tears down her cheeks.

The woman continued to smile. "Fear not, child. One so perseverant is to be rewarded. I will not kill you tonight. No. Tonight, you are my companion watching the fruits of my labor unfold here with me."

She removed her arm from Naomi's shoulder. Her muscles did not relax, and her shoulder still felt cold from the touch. "The dead are burying their dead tonight. But as for you, child, I want you to remember that it was I who let you go. I want you to go out and proclaim what you have seen here."

Naomi couldn't believe what she was hearing. Was she really being allowed to leave? A glimmer of hope cut through the chilling aura, some sense that maybe everything would be alright after all.

The woman's smile turned more sinister now. "I want them to know we exist. I want them to know that we are coming for them. I want them all to run. I want them all to flee. It will make the hunt more interesting for us. Tell them all that you have seen. And as you go, preach, saying, 'The kingdom of Hell is at hand.' For Hell is indeed at hand, little one, and your life is only fleetingly spared tonight."

Naomi felt hope extinguish within her quickly. She realized that she was being spared for a much worse tribulation: these vampires were here to stay. And they were going to spread like an apocalyptic plague of biblical proportions. Nowhere would be safe: not her home, not some hotel out-of-state, not even a place overseas. Naomi saw her life both beginning and ending in the same moment.

"You may want to hurry along," the woman said, still smiling that devilish grin. Motioning to the twitching officers on the ground, she said, "These will be waking soon. The ones inside may spot you and come after you, too. And I will not deny my newborn children an easy snack. So run along, child, and spread my good news."

At that, the woman bared her fangs in full and hissed at Naomi. Naomi screamed and ran away into the night. She didn't know where she was headed. Just far, far away from that horrible place.

The woman smiled and looked up at the moon. It was in its Waxing Gibbous phase.

TOBRIE

"I think someone's watching us."

Toby turned around. "What?"

Brie, who was lying under the sleeping bag, pointed at the partially open door. "I think I saw someone."

Toby walked over to the doorway and peeked out. The hallway was pitch black in either direction. Some moonlight seeped in through the broken windows and doorless rooms to illuminate cobwebs and floating dust, but he didn't see anybody.

"There's no one there," he said, going back to work on the opposite wall. "We're alone. Trust me."

"I'm pretty sure I saw someone," she said, pushing a few strands of brown hair behind her ear.

"Yeah? What'd they look like?" Toby said, shaking the can of white spray paint.

"I didn't get a great look," Brie said. "Just thought I saw a shadow move."

"Maybe it was a car passing by," Toby said. "Lights from the road or something."

"Maybe."

Toby was just like that. Even if there were someone there, he wouldn't care. He'd probably just invite them in for a smoke and start shooting the shit.

As she kept her ears open for any movement out in the hallway, Brie turned her attention back to Toby. The abandoned house was very dark, and this room was no exception, but her eyes had long since adjusted to the darkness. Silver streams of moonlight pierced through gaps in the wood boarding up the windows. The light caught his brown hair and made the rattail visible. She'd begged him to get rid of the rattail.

"You need a tan," she said, observing his bare ass. It was so pale that it was practically its own light source.

"I know," he laughed. He started spraying paint again.

It wasn't the worst idea, she decided. Breaking into the Newton House for a quickie, some blunts, and now Toby's revenge on their psychology professor immortalized in white spray paint on the wall. There were worse ways to spend Fall break.

I guess I won't break up with him just yet, she thought. *Still . . .*

"This place creeps me out," Brie said. Although she hadn't seen anything up here, she was sure she'd seen some spiders and possibly even a rat scurry away when they'd snuck in through the living room window. Her ears were alert for the sound of anything skittering around in the darkness.

"It's an old house," Toby said. "Probably just the dark playing tricks on your eyes. We'd hear anyone coming. The floor creaks so much, you couldn't sneak up those stairs without letting the whole house know."

"Yeah, I guess."

"There's no one there, Brie. We're good."

"But what if there is? What if some pervert is just watching us? Hiding in the dark waiting to attack or something?"

Toby stopped spraying the wall and turned to look at the partially ajar door. He looked uncertainly at the darkened hallway beyond. The only sound was a gentle wind outside. Neither said anything for a moment, waiting. Nothing happened. Toby finally shivered and said, "Well, shit, Brie, now you got me spooked. I'm imagining some monster just waiting out in the hall ready to jump out at us or something!"

She laughed, deciding that maybe she was just imagining things. "Maybe you should crawl back under here and protect me from the big, scary monster."

Toby laughed. "Alright, hang on." He finished spray-painting the wall. "There we are. My greatest masterpiece." The graffiti adorned the wall in brilliant white characters: *PROF. JENKINS SUX A$$*.

Toby flicked the wall off. "Give us an F, we'll give you the finger."

"Hang on," Brie said, getting up and walking over to the wall. Taking the can from him, she knelt down and started spray-painting underneath Toby's declaration.

"Whatcha doing?" Toby said.

"Just some finishing touches," Brie said, smiling. When she finished, she stepped back and leaned against Toby. Despite the cool air, his skin was warm and comforting. He put his arm around her bare waist and smiled at her contribution. The word *TOBRIE* was enclosed by a white heart.

"We really do have an adorable couple's name, don't we?" he said. She kissed his cheek, put the paint can on the floor, then leaped back into the sleeping bag.

"Okay, Van Gogh. Get your sexy ass back under here," Brie said, laughing and holding the covers open for him. Smiling at the view, Toby crawled back in with her. As they cuddled, he asked, "Whatcha wanna do now?"

She looked at him and wiggled her eyebrows suggestively. "Round two?"

"I don't know. I've got a headache coming on," he said.

"Probably from all the fumes," she said, motioning with her head towards the paint can.

"Yeah, probably."

"Well, what do *you* wanna do?"

He thought for a moment, then cupped her breast with his left hand. "Screw it. Round two it is."

He leaned in, and they began kissing. She pulled him on top of her and closed the blanket around them. As they started at it again, they heard a car pass by on the road outside. The floorboards beneath them creaked a little with each thrust. Other than that, it was quiet in the house.

"Shit!" Brie said, pulling away and sitting up suddenly.

"What?"

Brie pointed towards the door. "I *swear* I saw something this time."

"What'd you see?" Toby asked, scooting out from between her legs and looking at the door.

"*Eyes.*"

"Eyes? Babe, it's hella dark out there."

"I'm not kidding, Toby. I saw *glowing eyes.* Like little Christmas lights."

"Glowing eyes?" He laughed. "I didn't think you smoked that much."

She swatted his chest. "Dude! Seriously? There's someone out there!"

"Babe, there's no one out there."

"Go check."

"I just checked! There's no one there!"

"Jesus Christ, Toby."

She got up and quickly threw her blue shirt back on. She headed towards the door. Toby remained under the sleeping bag, enjoying the view of her body. The door creaked slightly as she opened it further and peered out.

"I don't see anything now," she said.

"Just close the door. There's no one out there," Toby said.

"I don't like this," Brie said. "Maybe we should head back."

Realizing that the mood was over, Toby groaned and rolled out of the sleeping bag. Standing up to put his underwear and jeans back on, he said, "There's nothing out there."

"Do you hear that?" she whispered.

"Hear what?"

"It sounds like hissing."

Midway through putting on his jeans, he stopped and listened. Sure enough, he could hear the hissing too. It sounded almost like a cat warning another animal to stay away.

"Do you see anything?" he asked.

"No."

"Here, let me see."

After zipping up his jeans, Toby walked over to the door. Brie backed away towards the sleeping bag. As he peered out, Brie started putting her underwear and pants back on.

Toby peered into the darkness. Although his eyes had adjusted to the dark, he couldn't make out anybody in the hallway. He saw the dark shapes of an old bookshelf and a chair sunken into a soft spot of the floor, probably from untended water damage long ago. Nothing seemed to stir in the rays of moonlight cutting through the windows.

Then it dawned on him: he was looking directly at the person Brie had seen. They were just as cloaked in darkness as anything else in the hallway, but when Toby stared really hard, he could make out two beady, glowing eyes. Their luminance was dim.

"What's up, home skillet? You lost?" Toby said, hoping to scare away whoever it was.

The last thing Toby saw was those beady, glowing eyes light up and glare back at him.

"What are you doing?" Brie asked, putting her socks back on now.

Before Toby could answer, a dark shape cloaked itself around him and slammed into him, shoving him back across the room and right into the tribute to Professor Jenkins. The dark figure covered him and pinned him to the wall. Before Brie could register what was happening, blood started spraying from between Toby and this shadowy thing. Toby let out a pained cry. Blood sprayed all over the graffiti.

She ran towards them to try and pull the person off of Toby, but the moment she grabbed them, the person turned around and roared at her with the ungodliest screech she'd ever heard. It was like something out of the amphitheater of Hell. It was a man's face. But he had long, sharp fangs, and his mouth dripped with blood.

Toby's blood.

The man's eyes glowed a vibrant white that felt as if they were commanding her to step back. In her sudden repulsion, Brie moved backwards and tripped on the sleeping bag. As she fell, her head slammed down on the floor, knocking her senseless. The last thing she recalled in that final moment before blacking out was the sound of Toby's horrible, awful screaming.

When she came to, all was silent.

It was still dark. She didn't know how long she'd been out. She was still on the floor. Reaching back behind her head, she felt a warm, matted part of her hair. She winced at the touch.

As her eyes adjusted to the dark, she realized that Toby was standing at the wall, staring at her. His body from the neck down was covered in dark blood. His neck had been opened, and the flow had draped over his chest, torso, and jeans like a shredded cloak. Yet he was still standing there, looking at her. He swayed a little bit, blinked even.

"Toby?" Brie said, vaguely hoping that the mysterious attacker had been defeated somehow. The attacker was nowhere to be seen.

Toby simply stared at Brie.

"Where'd he go?"

Toby walked over to Brie and leaned down. He slowly cupped her cheeks with his hands. Looking into his eyes, which were no longer green but rather a pale ring of white, she wasn't sure how to feel. Every inch of her wanted to run, wanted to get as far from this abandoned place as possible. This wasn't the same, lovable goofball she'd hooked up with over the summer. This was a confident stranger. He was strong, sexy, terrifying, and somehow his eyes told her that all was well, and that this would be over soon.

She didn't scream as Toby sank his fangs into her neck.

DEAD MAN'S CURVE

It was October 3rd, and twelve-year-old Alan Wolitzer searched frantically through the garage. There was his dad's tool bench—his mom hadn't touched it since the divorce—and the usual clutter of boxes, unfinished wood projects, loose nails, an uncoiled extension cable, and that hideously old, tar-caked tool cabinet.

Alan began opening the shelves, looking for two things: a box of screws and a drill. He found them both on the bottom shelf. Now he just needed wood.

Lots and lots of wood.

Did Mom even come home last night?

She usually parked the car here in the garage, but her car was gone. It wasn't even outside in the driveway. Morning sunlight poured in through the garage window, creating a glare on a small puddle of water in the spot where she normally parked.

Alan had worked with his dad on a lot of woodworking projects over the years: replacing the mailbox post, building the shed out back, assembling the old treehouse, fixing Lucky's doghouse (before she died). Whenever his dad needed spare wood, he'd grab some from underneath the tool bench. Wiping cold sweat from his forehead, Alan kneeled down and found a stack of 2x4s and plywood scraps. He wasn't sure if it'd be enough.

It'll have to do.

He was going to have to board up every window and entrance to the house as quickly as possible. He'd start with that garage window.

Going back through the kitchen door that connected to the garage, Alan turned left and peered through the dining room window once more to see if maybe his mom had returned yet. She hadn't.

He turned right and headed through the living room down towards his bedroom at the far end of the hallway. In his room, his bed was against the opposite wall adjacent to a bedstand with an alarm clock, a half-eaten plate of crackers he'd made for himself last night, the thermometer, and a washcloth that had long since dried out.

He couldn't remember if his mom came into his room to check on him or not last night. He'd gotten home and felt the shakes fall over him, so he'd crawled into bed with a wet washcloth and fallen asleep not long after.

She must've left for work already, he decided.

When he'd used the thermometer the night before, it had read 101.2. He'd hoped the soreness and chills were just a fluke that could be slept off because truthfully, he had been looking forward to going to school today. Derek had a new collection of milk caps he wanted to trade. And it was Tuesday, which meant library day with Mrs. Fitzgerald.

Jody was in Mrs. Fitzgerald's class.

He liked seeing Jody. She normally sat with a bunch of other girls whom he found intimidating, and so despite her beautiful long, black hair and tan skin, he was normally too chicken to try and talk to her. Jody hadn't been in class last week, so he'd been looking forward to today in the hopes of seeing her.

Everything changed, however, when he heard the news on the radio that morning.

The news about violent people overrunning the city hospital last night, escaping out into the streets, and attacking innocent bystanders chilled his already shaky bones. Several dozen people were reported missing. The hospital had apparently erupted into flames.

Gotta find Mom.

As Alan walked over to his bedstand, the clock read 11:02 AM. A commercial break for a new video game system that used CDs was playing on the radio. He unplugged the clock and took it with him back to the kitchen. His homeroom teacher, Mrs. Lenore, had taught about how back in the 20s, a bunch of people got sick up in Alaska, and they had to send for medicine that a bunch of dogs had to mush through snow and wilderness to get. She explained how back then, people communicated using radio, telegrams, older types of telephones, and Morse code. He and his classmates were asked to imagine how much easier they could communicate today with things like cellular phones and televised broadcasts.

This situation didn't look like it would need sled dogs, but it seemed that communication was going to be more important than ever, so he figured he'd better listen to the news while he got to work.

There was an island with a sink and dishwasher in the center of the kitchen. He plugged the clock into an outlet on the side of this island and set the clock on the countertop. The clock flashed 12:00, but he didn't bother changing it. He had more pressing tasks today.

It was already set to the station he wanted to listen to—he only ever listened to the same one—so he extended the antennae and swiveled it around until he found a decent signal. Mama MacDaddy's relaxing drawl came through staticky but clear.

". . . was found not guilty. This was just a little bit ago. Look, I'm not a legal expert. I'm not really into court drama stuff. Court stuff bores me! But I think the jury was smoking something if you know what I mean. There's no way in H-E-DOUBLE-HOCKEY-STICKS he's innocent. I can't believe they found him not guilty. Ridiculous! Anyway, let's move on because as soon as Randy Daddy-O gets back, we've got some updates on that crazy hospital story. It's really scary, to tell you the truth . . ."

Leaving the kitchen door open, Alan went back into the garage. He grabbed a sizable sheet of plywood, the drill, and some screws. He stumbled over to the garage window and rested for a moment. After all the projects he'd worked on with his dad, he was normally fine working with wood and even enjoyed it, but this sickness made it feel more like an endurance test than anything else. He took a few breaths, then lifted the plywood sheet up off the ground again. Moving past some boxes and a large, blue steamer trunk that used to belong to his grandma, Alan hoisted the plywood up clumsily to the window. It was awkward and bulky, but he managed to rest it on the windowsill and hold it in place long enough to begin drilling a screw into the bottom left corner.

The sunlight filtering through the window was now reduced, cutting through only at the top, uncovered portion of the window. He could hear the traffic outside going way too fast around the corner. He and Sam, the neighbor kid across the street, called it Dead Man's Curve because cars came around it so quickly. He had to cross it on his walks home from school. It wasn't safe to cross the street there.

It hadn't been safe to cross there yesterday.

He put a screw in the bottom right corner and decided that he needed a chair to reach the top sections safely. He looked around the garage for something to stand on.

Of all the things Dad took when he left, it had to be the ladders.

Leaning against the steps leading up to the kitchen door, he saw an old fold-up chair. He went to grab it, vaguely recalling some children's book his teacher read once that specifically warned against using folding chairs like ladders.

The radio sounded from the kitchen. "Well, folks, the world might be scary, but the show must go on. This is Mama MacDaddy, bringing you today's greatest hits with Mama MacDaddy's Mixtape! This next one is *da bomb*." The music resumed, but Alan was too distracted to really hum along. Setting up the chair, he climbed onto it and put two more screws in the top of the plywood.

Mom's gonna hate this. She'll thank me later, he thought.

After he finished screwing the plywood in place, Alan grabbed a 2x4 that looked long enough to cover the window's top section. Climbing back onto the chair and placing the 2x4 against the window frame, he drilled screws into it at both ends. He knew how important leveling and measuring were when it came to projects like this. That past spring, he'd helped his dad extend the back deck to include a space for a jacuzzi. However, time was not on his side right now. He had to make do with eyeballing it.

When he finished, he got down, grabbed the drill and box of screws, and headed back up the stairs to the kitchen. He stopped at the top of the stairs and turned, looking at the large garage door.

There's no way to board that up, he thought. *I guess it'll be too hard for anyone to break through without the opener. I'll leave it for now.*

He went inside the kitchen, closed the door behind him, and locked it.

He suddenly felt his energy leave him. He leaned on the kitchen island and took deep, slow breaths. Despite his urgency, his fever hadn't left him at all. He still felt weak and shaky, and boarding up the garage window had taken a lot out of him. But he couldn't stop now.

"Welcome back to Mama MacDaddy's Mixtape! I'm joined by Randy Daddy-O. We got some more details on this breaking story that started when the patients at a hospital in North Carolina overran the staff and started attacking. Killed everyone. No survivors that we've heard yet, not even the police who went to investigate. Eyewitnesses say the patients escaped into the neighborhoods and began attacking citizens, and now, last we heard, a reported fifty-six people are missing. What's the latest, Daddy-O?"

A man with a Southern drawl spoke with what Alan felt was a sobering tone compared to his usual *Aren't-I-just-a-loveable-hick* personality.

"Well, Mama, I wish I could tell the usual joke here, but it doesn't feel right, given the circumstances, ya know? I told you this mornin' it was fifty-six people missin'. That was the count this mornin'. It's actually risen now. It's a hundred and twenty-two people now."

"Oh God," Mama MacDaddy said, dropping her bubbly personality for the first time Alan could recall. He'd listened to this show in the mornings when his dad would drive him off to school. Mama MacDaddy and Randy Daddy-O were two playful goofs who greeted your mornings with music and jokes about current events. They were two North Carolinians he imagined he'd one day like to hang out with and crack jokes with. To him, they were just as much passengers in the car rides to school with his dad as he was. After the divorce, he continued listening to them. Their familiar and comforting voices reminded him of a simpler time when he didn't have to think about how much money was in the bank account, when he didn't have to walk home from school, when he didn't know that Melinda was anything more than his dad's coworker who sometimes needed rides home after work.

Their tone this episode was different. It was as if they were realizing, live on-air, just how serious the situation was.

"My cousin Benjamin, he's the officer I spoke to," Daddy-O continued. "He said the 9-1-1 calls are nonstop, more people bein' reported missin' left and right, more people gettin' attacked by deranged psychopaths. Lunatics runnin' around. Most of the attacks are people from the hospital, still in their hospital gowns. Some of them are just plain nekkid."

"What, like they lost their hospital gowns or something?" Mama MacDaddy said.

"Probably. But here's the thing. Now they're gettin' calls about people in everyday clothes attackin' people. People dressed like you and me. Overalls, jeans, skirts, dresses. Not the hospital folks. Regular people. They go around. They're snarlin' and bitin' people on the necks, sometimes tearin' people to shreds."

"Jesus Christ."

Alan looked up, breathing slowly and trying not to panic. He started counting how many windows were in the house. The dining room to his left was nothing more than a small inlet with a large window overlooking the driveway and side yard. Opposite him was the living room. There was a huge, sliding backdoor and two other windows.

Beyond the kitchen wall to his right was the foyer with the front door, which had two narrow windows running alongside it. They were still wide enough for someone to break and enter through.

His eyes followed to the hallway leading to the bedrooms. He knew the guest bedroom, his bedroom, and his mom's bedroom each had large windows. His mom's room had its own bathroom with an additional smaller window.

He needed to seal up every entrance. He went back to the garage for more wood.

"It's like some sort of communicable disease, ya know? Benji said this one lady collapsed near the downtown library. They saw she had bite marks on her, so they called the medics. Now they couldn't take her to the hospital, obviously. The thing's up in flames. So they try to go twenty minutes down the road to another one. But the ambulance truck never made it. Benji said he and his partner went out to investigate the missin' truck, right? And so they found it flipped over on its side in a ditch. Said there was nobody inside. Now get this. There were bloody slash marks everywhere. Seat all tore up, windows smashed, blood everywhere. But no bodies. And so those three paramedics and the lady are also missin' now."

"You said people are getting bit on their necks?" Mama MacDaddy chimed in.

"Bit. Tore up. That's what he said the 9-1-1 calls are makin' it sound like."

"It's . . . it's vampirism!" Mama MacDaddy now

sounded genuinely scared.

Alan's stomach cramped, and drowsiness made his head throb.

"What's that?" Randy Daddy-O asked.

"It's vampires! They're vampires! They bite you. You turn into a vampire. You bite someone else. That person turns into a vampire. It's like a plague of vampirism. It's a literal epidemic, a disease that's gonna keep spreading."

"Vampires? Like Dracula?" Daddy-O asked, trying to keep things light but still clearly concerned.

"Dracula on crack, maybe. Like Dracula meets the Bubonic Plague. God, this has to be a sick joke, right?"

"I wish I could say it was, but it ain't, Mama. That hospital was reported bein' on fire, last Benji told me, but the details are still fuzzy. People really have gone missin', and the 9-1-1 lines are clogged worse than my Uncle Aaron's arteries."

Vampires.

He hadn't wanted to say the word when he first woke up to the news of hospital patients escaping into the night biting people. He knew vampires weren't real. His first thoughts were that it was some elaborate prank. It was October, after all. It was the time of year for spooky pranks. When it became clear the reports were serious, however, and there really were people being bitten and turned into ravenous monsters themselves, he realized the word was the only appropriate one to describe the situation. And that meant that everybody was in serious danger.

As Alan walked back into the kitchen carrying an armful of cut-up 2x4s, he stopped and rested at the counter again. Setting the wood down, he leaned on the island and took deep breaths. His aches were wearing him out.

Water.

He poured a cup of water from the sink and gulped it down. The water didn't seem to quench his lungs as much as he'd hoped. He looked over at the TV set where his video game system was. The controller was still left out, uncoiled and easy to trip on. Just the other day he'd been playing a game that was about traveling across Europe and killing monsters with a spear. He'd just made it to the Leaning Tower of Pisa level. The game was scary and fun.

But this was not fun. That these things might actually exist was far more horrifying than any video game.

He went back into the garage and grabbed more wood: squares and rectangles of plywood, 1x4 and 2x4 scraps, and even a few pieces that once served as panels on old furniture. It wouldn't be enough wood for the whole house, but he figured he could probably use heavy furniture in some of the rooms.

Gotta board up what I can.

He made several trips between the garage and kitchen island, dumping the wood on the countertop and going back for more. He wondered what Jody would've thought if she could see him now working so hard while being so weak and sick. When he finally had all the wood he could find, he grabbed the drill

92

and started boarding up the window in the dining room. His muscles felt weak, and it was purely forcing his arms to move that got the window boarded up at all. The kitchen became visibly dimmer once he finished blocking off the entire window. He flicked the kitchen light on, but somehow this didn't seem to do much. If anything, the light was muted. It just didn't look right to him.

He moved over to the sliding back door in the living room. This was going to be the hardest one to close off. Overlooking the backyard, the two glass doors were much longer than any of the scrap wood he'd found.

Gotta use furniture for this one, he thought.

Looking over to his left, he eyed two bookcases in the far corner. He contemplated how best to use them. They both looked long enough to cover the expanse of the doors. He imagined simply moving them in front of the doors, then he realized he could stack them on their sides. *If I stack them longways and on top of each other, that'll cover most of the doorway.*

He walked to the bookcases and started taking books off of them. He set the books in little piles behind the couch so he could move the bookcases over once he finished.

I feel so drugged.

He dragged the first bookcase over to the sliding doors and laid it down on its side. It just barely reached the plaster on either side of the glass doorway. Then he realized that the bookcase's backside was just flimsy cardboard. The slightest kick would break through it.

He looked around. There had to be some sort of an alternative.

Then he had an idea.

The books. Then the couch.

He could stack the other bookcase on top, then screw the two bookcases together. Then, for added weight and support for the flimsy backs, he could put the stacks of books back on the shelves. Lastly, he would push the couch in front of the whole mess. The couch's rubber legs made it nearly impossible to push against the carpeted floor.

That might actually work.

He grabbed the other bookcase and dragged it on top of the other. The task normally wouldn't have taken so much energy out of him, but he felt faint and dizzy.

Can't stop now. Keep going, man.

Grabbing the drill, he screwed the two bookcases together. When he was finished, he shook the structure to check how well the screws connected them. Satisfied, he began grabbing the books and stacking them on the sideways bookcases. When he finished stacking the books, he shook the structure once more. It felt much heavier now, so he mustered his strength to move the couch against it. He had to lift one end of the couch and swivel it towards the bookcases, then go to the other side and repeat this action. He soon had the back door sufficiently blocked off. There was about a two-foot-wide gap of window at the top exposed, but he had no way to block that off just now.

Mom might have an idea when she gets back from work.

Someone started beating on the front door.

A wave of panic shot through him, and the instinct to run washed over him.

"Hello? Anyone in there?" It was a man.

It's him. He's come back.

Alan clutched the drill and darted over to the kitchen island. Mama MacDaddy was in disbelief about a report that someone in the studio had gone missing. Alan turned the volume down and snuck over to the kitchen wall.

Peeking around the corner into the foyer, he saw that a man was peering in through the front door windows. Alan quickly hid back behind the kitchen wall, hoping to God that he hadn't been seen.

"Hey, if anyone's in there, you need to evacuate! We're all headed towards a safe zone over in Raleigh!" It didn't sound like the man from yesterday. This guy spoke frantically and in a hurry. The man yesterday had been different.

He'd acted different. Lots of hissing and shrieking. No words.

Alan finally dared another peek around the corner. The man was gone.

These windows next, he thought.

Because they were narrow and rectangular, he was able to put up two long 2x4s running vertically on each of them. Once he finished, he screwed three more 2x4s across the top, middle, and bottom of the front door to block it from being opened.

Walking back into the living room, he stumbled. Dropping the drill, he fell to the floor this time.

I'm so weak, man. I can't walk. I gotta rest. Why is my mouth so dry?

He forced himself up and over to the kitchen. Grabbing his glass of water, he filled it up and drank it whole. Then he filled it up again. And again. And again. After four whole glasses, his belly felt full, but his mouth still felt as dry as cotton.

I don't feel so good.

But he had to keep moving.

His mind swirled with thoughts about the radio reports. The hospital. The disappearances. The attacks. People fighting back. It sounded like they were using whatever they could: guns, knives, baseball bats, their fists. Mama MacDaddy and Daddy-O started talking about making stakes and selling them. Daddy-O joked that they could make a fortune. Mama laughed nervously.

Even though they were trying to keep things light, Alan knew the world was falling apart outside.

Mom.

He forced himself up and over to the kitchen. On the wall near the garage doorway was the phone. Underneath it was a notepad with several numbers: Mom's work, Mom's pager, Mom's car phone, Dad's work, Dad's pager. His mom hadn't had a chance to erase his dad's numbers yet. Picking up the receiver, he tried his mom's car phone.

There was no answer.

He tried her work number.

This took him to a busy signal that ended the call all together. He tried her work number again, but he only got the busy signal again.

Mom, please call me back.

He sent the house number to her pager and hung up, now thoroughly exhausted and worried that his mom might not have come home at all last night. He remembered tossing and turning fitfully throughout the night, but he couldn't recall hearing her come home or seeing her check in on him. The more he thought about it, he couldn't even recall falling asleep or climbing into bed. All he could remember were the nightmares. And the man's face.

The man from yesterday.

His eyes had paralyzed Alan with fear when he saw him on the street. He kept seeing those eyes in the dark shadows of his room, through the partially moonlit windows, and in his nightmare.

His nightmare had been simple. He was in his room, but there was no moonlight to illuminate it. Everything was pitch black except those eyes of the man who'd attacked him yesterday on the way home from school.

Alan opened his eyes. He remembered hanging up the telephone, but now he was lying on the floor next to the island. He didn't remember getting there. The already greatly dimmed house was even darker as the orange light of late afternoon poured in through the tops of the sliding glass doors.

How long have I been lying here?

He stood up slowly, still feeling incredibly weak. His stomach ached as if he hadn't eaten anything in months. And his mouth was painfully dry.

He went back over to the phone. He tried calling his mom again. First the car phone. Then her work number. Both times, he got the busy signal.

Desperate, he called his dad's work. Same thing: busy signal.

He called 9-1-1.

Busy signal.

Hanging up, he looked at the living room. There were still the two other windows in the area behind the dining room. Grabbing the drill and some wood, he stumbled over there. He was weak, but he had to board up the house. He had to make sure no one could get in or out.

As he screwed a 1x4 across the top of the left window, he heard someone scream outside.

It came from somewhere down the road.

He ignored the scream, grabbed another screw, and began drilling in another 2x4.

Suddenly someone was beating on the front door again.

"Is there anybody in there?" a man shouted. He was sure it wasn't the same man as before or even the one from yesterday, but his mind couldn't focus on that now. A wave of exhaustion started dragging him down. Alan saw the drill fall from his hand, and suddenly he was on the floor as well.

No, not quite exhaustion.

It was hunger.

I'm so hungry, he thought. He wondered what he could grab to eat from the cabinets. He ran through everything he had eaten that day: crackers, water . . .

That was it. Crackers and water. Neither had done much for him. If he'd really gone that long without eating anything, it was no wonder why he felt so weak. Maybe a sandwich or something from the fridge might help. But the more he thought about it, the less he really wanted anything from the kitchen. The idea of eating just made him feel sicker.

It was going on late afternoon, that was clear, but how had it slipped by so quickly? It seemed like it was morning just moments ago.

I can't keep track of time. What's wrong with me?

Alan sat up, determination sweeping through him.

I've got to finish.

He grabbed another 2x4, then thought to himself, *I haven't even started on the bedrooms!* Picking up the drill and box of screws, he lugged the 2x4 with him down the hallway. As he passed his mom's room, he thought to himself, *I can save wood if I just board up her door. Don't need to go in there, anyway.*

Once in his room, he realized how big his window was. *Gonna need a lot more wood for this one.* He turned and went back to the kitchen. Once there, he saw the exposed windows in the living room again and panicked.

I've been at this all day and I'm nowhere close to finished!

Another scream came from outside. This one sounded closer.

He hastily grabbed a 2x4 and propped it up against one of the living room windows. He reached for his drill only to remember that he'd left it in the bedroom.

I'm supposed to board up my bedroom. He dropped the 2x4 on the floor as his mind swirled with multiple tasks that all needed doing at that exact moment. It was all starting to blend in his mind, a fleeting slosh of images as disorganized as his sense of time had become.

Bedroom window . . . living room window . . . bedroom . . . Mom's room . . .

Dizzy, he fell to the floor again. He didn't lose consciousness this time, though.

Why can't I focus?

Trying to think more clearly, he sat up. He saw his backpack on the kitchen table.

I missed the library today. I didn't get to see Jody today.

He felt a tear trickle down his cheek. He began to accept that he would probably never see Jody again.

Knocking on the door. This one sounded more frantic than before. "Please let us in! It's getting dark outside! They're everywhere! We've got no place to go!" A man's voice.

Alan stood up and looked at the bookshelf structure he'd assembled against the sliding glass doors. Now he realized that despite all his efforts in putting it together, any reasonably determined person could probably break it down and enter.

Or escape.

He heard pushing at the front door. Someone was trying to get in.

"It won't budge!"

He heard glass shatter and someone trying to kick in the wood covering the front door windows.

"Someone's boarded this place up."

"Let's try the back," another voice said. It was another man.

Alan stood up, suddenly too hungry to care about intruders. His stomach was cramped, and his mouth was so dry. He leaned over on the kitchen island. Only now did he realize that the alarm clock radio was still playing. A man was speaking in a serious tone. Mama MacDaddy's Mixtape would have ended hours ago.

". . . urging everyone living in and around the affected areas to head west. Safe zone camps for evacuees have begun appearing. There's a camp in Raleigh and a relief camp in Greensboro. Officials have not confirmed their plans to resolve this crisis but are in the preliminary stages of a response. I can confirm that they are investigating the emergency. We have reports that military vehicles have begun assembling, though they have not yet been deployed into the affected areas. Officials say they are awaiting a direct order to . . ."

So much noise.

Alan moved toward the radio to turn it off.

". . . seem to possess superhuman strength and speed. Some reports indicate they can pass through walls, almost like ghosts. Physical attacks have been shown to have some effect, however, as witnesses say . . ."

Alan shut the radio off.

He was now keenly aware of the two men walking outside near the garage door towards the dining room window.

Dead Man's Curve, he thought. The road outside the house. The road he had to cross to get to his house. The road where the man had been.

It came to Alan in fleeting images as he rested against the kitchen island. The man was old and frail, dressed for Church (even though it had been Monday), and he looked lost just standing there in the middle of the road.

He didn't look like he was from the hospital. Couldn't have been from the hospital. This was before the hospital thing. Where are they coming from?

Alan had instinctively kept closer to the left sidewalk leading into his neighborhood. He wanted to shout to the man to get out of the road, that someone could come speeding around the corner and hit him, but he didn't know the man and didn't want to end up on the six o'clock news.

The man didn't appear to know where he was. He just stood there and looked blankly at the trees.

When Alan crossed over to the right where his house was, the man saw him and sprang at him with shocking speed. He grabbed Alan and then . . .

The two men outside walked through the small shrubs lining the front of the house.

"I think someone's got this place boarded up tight. Look! More boards on the garage window."

"Those bedrooms don't look boarded up."

"Yeah, but they're kinda high off the ground. Maybe a ladder?

"No. Maybe the garage, but it's boarded up. Wanna try another house?"

"Maybe. Let's walk around back and see if we can find another way in."

When Alan had encountered the man at Dead Man's Curve, he managed to get away. The man had an uncanny strength for his age, but Alan was able to use his weight to fall on the man's legs and break them. He heard the sickening crack of bone and rolled away onto the asphalt as the man howled a terrible cry. He sounded less like an old man yelling and more like one of the monsters from Alan's video games.

Alan could feel two streams of blood pulsing out from his neck where the man had bitten him. Looking down, he saw the streams had already bloodied his shirt. He went to stand up but fell underneath the shock of seeing so much of his own blood and hit his head on the curb. The impact knocked him out instantly.

When he awoke, he wasn't sure how much time had passed. It still looked like late afternoon. The blood had caked onto his shirt. Looking around, he didn't see the man.

That was when the sickness fell upon Alan. Standing up, he went inside and cleaned himself with a shower and change of clothes. He'd felt so sick that the thought of calling 9-1-1 to report the attack didn't even cross his mind.

I'll tell Mom when she gets home, he thought. *She'll know what to do.*

He'd gone to bed with his fever and the nightmares, not realizing that when she'd dropped him off for school that morning, it was the last time he would ever see her.

Alan finally accepted why his head was throbbing so hard now, why his body felt so weak. His body yearned for sustenance. Crackers and water would never do anything for him ever again.

He stood up from the kitchen island and stared at the boarded-up dining room window. He could hear the two men walking past it outside. They were heading towards the uncovered living room windows.

"Hey! Maybe we can get in through here!" he heard one of them say.

I'm so . . . thirsty.

Instinctively, he walked towards the wall. His thirst drove him forward, and before he could think about it too long, he walked straight through the wall like a ghost. He stood now in the shrubs lining the side yard of the house. The window behind him was still boarded up and untouched.

He turned and saw the two men on his right. One was a short, squat white man with no hair. The other was a taller, lean, Asian man. Both were dressed in their white shirts and ties with dark business pants. They looked like the Mormon missionaries who sometimes visited. Neither one noticed the young boy standing there as they peered into the window.

"Here, I'll push up from the bottom, and you try to work the top," the tall one said.

As they began working on opening the window, Alan felt his strength begin to muster. The murky thoughts swirled through his brain.

He'd just walked through a wall.

That's a pretty cool trick, he thought. *Could the old man do that? Did he know he could do that? If he could, why didn't he do it when I broke his legs? Can I do it again?*

His thoughts returned to his hunger. The hunger was not weakening him, he realized. It was giving him focus. A focus he'd never had before. A focus he'd never had in . . . in . . .

Math? Science? He couldn't really remember what classes he was taking. The memories were already becoming fuzzy. He knew he wanted to go to Mrs. Storytime's class, see Jenny.

No. That's not her name.

He remembered her face. He couldn't remember her name. He accepted that he'd never see her again.

And that thought made him angry.

The anger drove him forward faster than he ever remembered running. He pounced on the shorter man first, sinking his teeth into the man's throat, just as the old man had done to him yesterday.

He instantly felt the sickness begin to wane. His headache lessened, his stomach relaxed, and his mouth felt quenched. As the man screamed in surprise and agony, Alan tasted the blood as it flowed throughout his body, giving him strength. He'd never felt so powerful.

The other man screamed and started to run. Alan was sure he'd never felt so hungry in all his life. He sucked the man's blood greedily. He couldn't believe this is what he'd been boarding himself up to escape. This was far from an unpleasant nightmare.

He looked up and began to chase after the tall man who ran down the driveway to the left towards

Dead Man's Curve.

The man never made it beyond Dead Man's Curve.

THE LAST STAND OF RITA AND ESME

"Did you hear about that hospital over in Goldsboro?"

Esme was on her hands and knees pulling up weeds from the small garden of carrots that lined the front porch. She figured they had about another week or two before the garden closed up shop for the colder season. She turned around to see Rita standing behind her looking anxious against the cloudy sky.

"No, what happened?"

"They've been talkin' about it all day on the radio," Rita said, folding her arms. "A bunch of the hospital patients started actin' crazy and attackin' people. Bitin' the doctors and rippin' their throats out and shit."

"Jesus Christ," Esme said, returning to the weeding. "This for real?"

"Yeah, and apparently a lot of people have gone missin'."

"The police handle it?" Esme asked.

"Well, they sent the police in, but the police never came back!" Rita said, eyes wide with concern.

"Where's this happenin' at?"

"Over near Goldsboro."

Esme pulled out an especially big, thorny weed and tossed it aside. "Well, that's a good ways away from here," she said, standing up and taking off her gloves. She decided to take a break.

They lived in a two-story cabin situated on a mountainside overlooking a valley of mountains near Bostic, North Carolina. Their closest neighbor was two miles down the road. Aside from the small backroad that led through their neighborhood, they were surrounded by forests and mountains on all sides. Goldsboro was at least a four-hour's drive east of them.

"Whatever craziness is goin' on over there, I'm sure they'll get it figured out," Esme said.

"I don't know. They're already reportin' fifty-six missin' since last night," Rita said.

"Goddamn, that's a lot of people," Esme said. "I'm gonna take a break."

It was October 3rd, and as they sat at their kitchen table sipping lemonade while watching the news on the portable TV, Esme soon realized how serious the situation was.

". . . reports that the patients escaped into the streets. We have eye-witness reports and forthcoming video footage of several patients violently attacking citizens," the news anchor said while showing aerial footage of the hospital itself. The building was now a large mess of rubble devoured in black smoke and fire. Esme wondered why there weren't any firefighters putting it out.

"So, they just let it burn to the ground? That's gonna give the conspiracy whackos a lot of food to chew on," Esme chuckled, trying to keep things light. Rita, still nervous, chuckled along.

"Sounds an awful lot like vampires to me," Rita said.

"Whatcha mean?" Esme asked, finishing her lemonade and getting up for a refill.

Rita pointed at the television. "I mean, they bite people, and then those people start attackin' other people? Hello! It's like somethin' out of a goddamn horror movie! They're straight up vampires!"

"Vampires," Esme said to herself as she poured more lemonade. "That's horseshit."

But even as she turned around to face the television again, the news anchor said, "We have spoken with law enforcement who are actively investigating this rash of attacks and disappearances. Law officials say that we now have a reported four-hundred and seventeen missing people. Law enforcement is advising everyone in Wayne County and the surrounding counties to gather their families and evacuate until this crisis can be resolved. Evacuation camps have been established in Raleigh and Greensboro. This evacuation is advised for the following counties: Wilson, Greene, Johnston . . ."

"It's vampires, you dumbass! Just say the word! Vampires!" Rita shouted at the television.

"Vampires ain't real, Rita. He's not gonna say that," Esme said.

Rita threw up her hands. "This looks pretty

fuckin' real to me."

"Yeah, yeah. I guess it does," Esme agreed. "I wish they'd show a video of one of these attacks or somethin'. Get a better look at it."

Both watched in silence as the news anchor continued to list police warnings and updates on the number of missing people. Each time the news came back to the list of those missing, it seemed to increase by about fifteen.

"What if it comes here?" Esme asked.

Rita sighed. "That's why I'm worried. Goldsboro's kinda far away. But not that far."

"Hmm," Esme said, looking at her lemonade. It no longer tasted quite as good.

"We'll have to get stakes or somethin'," Rita said, her eyes still glued to the television.

"Well, hopefully they'll figure it out and get it under control," Esme responded. She poured her cup out in the sink, grabbed her gardening gloves, and went back outside to finish weeding.

Whatever control Esme thought possible was thoroughly eradicated by the next day, October 4th. On virtually every news channel, reports of over three-thousand missing people were always accompanied with the message, "Goldsboro has gone dark."

Rita and Esme came to understand that this meant no more news was coming out of Goldsboro. Whatever had happened, it was really bad, and now missing reports came in from as far north of

Goldsboro as Elm City, as far south as Rose Hill, as far east as Vanceboro, and as far west as Smithfield. Whatever this was, it was spreading. It was moving closer. And more people were going missing.

That afternoon, as they ate ham and cheese sandwiches with lettuce and freshly grown tomatoes, they watched the television, transfixed by the video that all the major networks had been playing.

Over in Selma, a man named Patrick Hughley had been filming his nephew's birthday party. The party was in someone's backyard. A man jumped over the wooden fence as one of the moms served cake, shrieked an awful yell that made the video's sound pop, then bit one of the children on the neck.

"What the fuck?" the cameraman shouted. The profanity was censored by the news, which Rita and Esme both thought was a ridiculous formality to worry about at this point. Patrick, shaking the camera mercilessly as he ran, dashed over to the kid. The children screamed as several other adults raced to pull the man off of the child, but the man lunged back, snarled, and shoved them all off. Then he leaped up and sank his fangs into one of the moms. At this point, everyone was running including the cameraman.

"Start the truck, Wayne! Start the truck!" he shouted, running into a blue truck with the camcorder at his side. He clearly wasn't trying to aim the camera anymore as the video only showed a shaky perspective of the concrete driveway as he ran.

"Jesus, I'm gonna be sick," Esme said, looking away from the shaky footage.

"Pick up the damn camera, dude! All I see is the friggin' asphalt!" Rita complained. The footage was dizzying to look at, but the screams in the background made it hard to look away.

"What the hell?" the driver shouted. At this point in the video, the cameraman realized he still had the camcorder on and mercifully pointed it to look through the truck's rear window. The video showed people hovering over multiple bodies in the streets. Their fangs were embedded in the peoples' necks, and they looked to be sucking on their necks with a sort of religious ecstasy.

"Jesus H. Christ," Esme said.

"What did I say! Fuckin' vampires," Rita said.

"Oh my God, oh my God, what the hell is this?" the cameraman kept saying. As soon as Wayne started the truck, one of the vampires looked up at the camera and shrieked that same, hideous yell that cracked the audio. His eyes glowed unnaturally bright, and then he launched into an inhumanly fast sprint towards the truck.

"Go! Go! Go!" Patrick shouted as Wayne floored the truck through the neighborhood. But the person seemed more than capable of keeping pace with the truck. It was only after the vampire—Esme decided calling him a vampire really was the best description —found someone else on the street to jump that Patrick and Wayne managed to get away.

After the video footage, more calls for evacuations in the surrounding areas were made. "Additional safety zones have now been established in Sanford,

Winston-Salem, Fayetteville, and Charlotte to assist travelers. The governor is advising citizens near the affected areas to relocate their families to the nearest safe zone for assistance. Evacuees are being told to take only what you need. Do not delay. This is an unprecedented crisis. Get out now. We've also been told that the president has been briefed on the situation. He has not made a public comment on the situation at this time."

"I'm goin' into town," Rita said suddenly, standing up and moving over to the counter.

"What for?" Esme said.

"Ammo. Bullets. Shells. Water and food, too, I guess."

"I'm sure they'll get this under control," Esme said, not even believing that herself.

"Es, this thing's movin'. Eventually, it's gonna come here." Rita grabbed the car keys dangling from the key holder over the kitchen counter. "I wanna be ready. Besides, I ain't up for movin' to some faraway place. This is our home. Least we can do is ride it out and defend it."

Esme smiled. "Goddamn it, you're right. Okay. What can I do?"

"Keep an eye on the news, see if anythin' happens." Rita grabbed her jacket off the coatrack and put it on. "I better hurry. Roy's good about keepin' stocked up, but if someone else got the same idea, he might be sold out already."

"Grab some eggs while you're out. Oh, and get some cheese and bread, too," Esme said.

"Any preferences?"

"Wheat and American."

With that, Rita left out the front door, hopped in their truck, and took off down the road.

That evening, they remained glued to the television set while enjoying the quiche Esme made. The reports moved on from the ever-rising numbers of missing people to the traffic jams and evacuation efforts. It was announced that the president was expected to make an announcement, but an interview with someone who had escaped the hospital in Goldsboro was set to air at six o'clock first. Recording from an undisclosed location somewhere outside of Blowing Rock, the six o'clock team interviewed a teenage girl named Naomi Perry.

When the interview started, Esme immediately noticed the girl's thousand-yard stare.

"Looks like she's been to Hell and back again," Esme said.

"Looks like she wants to get outta there,' Rita said, taking another bite of the quiche.

In fact, Naomi looked ready to run at the sound of a needle dropping. She detailed her harrowing escape from the hospital that had been overrun by vampires.

Rita clapped her hands and said, "Thank you! Finally, someone callin' it what it is!"

Naomi explained that this was a vampiric plague in the making. All of the missing people were gone because they had been attacked by actual vampires. Many of them probably were vampires now, as had happened in the hospital. She didn't know how to stop them. She said there was an evil woman who started it. She didn't know her name.

"Now you're talking about the people becoming vampires," the reporter interviewing Naomi said in a tone that implied skepticism. "We've certainly heard that expression come up in the newsroom, but most people don't believe in vampires. And we don't really have any video footage of what went on in that hospital. We know a fire broke out and it burned down, and the emergency teams sent to handle it have all disappeared. What would you say to the people who find that what you're saying is hard to believe?"

Naomi closed her eyes.

"I don't give a fuck who believes me," the girl said firmly.

Esme laughed. "Well, they didn't censor that one!"

"Everyone needs to be getting as far away from these things as possible," Naomi continued.

"To the safe zones, you mean?"

Naomi shook her head furiously. "No. Further. We need to get out of here. We shouldn't even be doing this interview here. We all need to get out. These things are coming for everyone. Everywhere."

"So, you're saying we should go somewhere far west of here? Like California?"

Naomi looked bewildered. "As far away as possible!"

"Well, now," the reporter said, trying to maintain an air of calm, "we have had reports of potential military intervention. The president hasn't announced it yet, but it seems safe to assume that's what his announcement will be later today."

Naomi kept shaking her head. "They're all going to die! We need to get out of here!"

"Plus," the reporter continued, "we do have local law enforcement in the affected areas, so we just need to evacuate to the safe zones and trust that they can do their jobs."

"They're already dead! They're already turned!" Naomi said frantically. "People need to be getting as far away from these things as possible." She then stood up, took the microphone off, and headed to the door.

"Wait, Miss Perry! We have more questions!" the reporter shouted from behind the camera. But the girl was gone.

Rita looked at Esme. "That girl knows what's up."

Esme nodded. "Sure you wanna ride this thing out still?"

"Yes. I need to call my sister, though."

Rita went over to the phone and started dialing a number.

"I thought Bella moved? She's not still in Goldsboro, is she?"

"No, she moved to Wendell. But that's not far from there."

"Okay."

The phone just gave Rita a busy signal.

An hour later, the President addressed the nation with a televised conference. He reassured the American people that he had already deployed troops with more on the way to handle the situation. He was confident that the crisis would come under control very soon.

Rita hadn't said anything after her failed attempt at reaching her sister.

As they watched, Esme kept replaying Naomi's words in her mind.

They're all going to die! They're all going to die!

After the speech, Rita and Esme went to bed. Esme hoped the girl on the news was wrong.

Things only got worse over the next few days.

On October 5th, areas near Wrightsville Beach, North Myrtle Beach in South Carolina, and Bracey in Virginia all went dark. Although several million North Carolinians had evacuated, reports were now coming out that the attacks had reached Chapel Hill.

As Rita weeded the tomato garden out back, she listened to the radio. There was no denying that the thing was spreading now. She was a little relieved to learn that troops had arrived in Raleigh. The reporter promised more details as they came in.

"Hey, Esme!" she called up to the cabin. A few moments later Esme appeared on the balcony about twelve feet above Rita's head.

"What?"

"I think we should go ahead and load the guns.

Just in case."

Esme didn't say anything at first. She just looked down, then up across the valley. Shielding her eyes from the overhead sun, she stared wistfully at the mountains surrounding them. It was bright and sunny with a few cumulus clouds today. Under ordinary circumstances, she'd have considered it a nice day out.

Esme sighed. "Alright." She went back inside.

On her way to the bedroom, she saw helicopter news footage on the TV of armed troops marching into Raleigh neighborhoods. Once in the bedroom, she opened their closet door. There was a tall, steel safe with a lock on it. Once she put in the combination 03031986 (the date she and Rita first broke ground in building this cabin), she opened it to take out their guns.

There were two double-barreled shotguns (one for each person) and seven handguns. Many of the shells and bullets Rita had purchased were on the bottom shelf of this safe. She pulled out the shotguns, the handguns, the bullets, two shell belts, and set it all out on the bed. Closing the safe, she started with the shotguns. After loading each barrel of the shotguns, she stuffed shells into the pockets of the shell belts. She had to smile.

Never thought I'd be gearin' up for an actual shootout.

Once she finished with the shotguns, she took the remaining shells to the kitchen table where Rita had left the rifle ammunition. Going back into the bedroom, she loaded the clips to each handgun. Each one could hold eight rounds. Once she finished, she took the remaining bullet boxes to the kitchen table.

Then she went to load the hunting rifles. They had two rifles, and each one could hold four cartridges. She loaded these up, then took them over to the kitchen table. Then she brought all the loaded weapons out from the bedroom and placed them on the table. She pointed them all away from the living room and towards the wall.

Going back outside, she called, "Guns're all on the kitchen table, good an' loaded."

Rita stood up with a basket full of tomatoes. "How's spaghetti sound tonight?"

"Sounds good to me."

The next day, Friday, they noticed several of the local stations were off the air. Each channel they flipped to had a screen that read *PLEASE STAND BY DUE TO TECHNICAL DIFFICULTIES* accompanied by a shrill, humming sound.

As Esme flipped through the channels, Rita came around the corner covering her ears. "Jesus Christ, turn the volume down! It's makin' my ears bleed!"

Esme turned the volume down.

"All the channels are out," Esme said.

"All of 'em?"

They found that the national channels were still broadcasting. According to the national news, many of the North Carolina media affiliates had gone dark. Attacks in Charlotte and Appomattox were reported before news crews opted to evacuate those areas. An order came down to ground all flights going in and out of North Carolina until this crisis could be brought under control. The last airplanes to depart before the order came down all left before noon.

That evening, the anchor on the six o'clock news announced, "More troops have been deployed as the entire battalion that marched through Raleigh has gone missing."

"What the fuck!" Rita shouted. They were both having mashed potatoes, green beans, and honeyed ham over TV trays on the couch. Looking at Esme, she said, "That girl was right. We're fucked!"

"Maybe," Esme said. She looked at the guns on the table.

"Military officials have confirmed that they lost contact with the battalion of over three hundred on-the-ground soldiers around three AM this morning," the news anchor continued. "Reports of heavy gunfire in the area were given at that time, but once the firing stopped, officials say they could not reach the soldiers through either visual means or through radio. It now appears that much of North Carolina, parts of South Carolina, and parts of Virginia have gone dark. The local news affiliates in those areas have since evacuated."

"Do you think the guns will be enough?" Esme asked.

"I sure as shit hope so," Rita said. "We've certainly got enough bullets to outlast Jesus's millennium kingdom."

"I know, but they're vampires," Esme continued.

"Shouldn't we get some wooden stakes or somethin'? Crosses?"

Rita thought for a moment. "Tell you what. I think we've got an old cross in a box somewhere. I'll find it. Then we can sharpen our walkin' sticks into long spears. We can shoot 'em in the head, then stab 'em with the spears. See if they come back after that."

Esme ate silently, pondering this strategy. "We are pretty remote in the mountains. Maybe they'll miss us entirely," she said, hoping this would be true. "Seems like they're goin' for the big cities."

Rita did not reply and fell quiet.

The news anchor droned on, unable to hide his emotional detachment from the situation. It was as if his method of maintaining composure at a time like this was to deny the existence of any emotions at all. "The president, speaking from a private bunker, continued to urge citizens to evacuate to western regions beyond the Mississippi River while the government handles this crisis. He reminded citizens to not seek out the former safe zones that were established as they are no longer safe. He also stated— excuse me—*restated* his position from earlier that nuclear weapons were not being considered at this time, which was a concern some had expressed. Here is the tape of that speech from earlier."

While the president spoke about innocent survivors in hiding and how ground-tactics would be better for them than the environmentally disastrous nuclear option, Esme looked at Rita.

"We really are in the thick of it now."

Rita was silent at first. Then, looking down at her food, she asked, "You think Bella got out?"

It was the first time she'd mentioned her sister since the failed phone call.

"I'm sure she got out as soon as they started tellin' people to evacuate. She's a smart woman," Esme said.

Rita didn't reply but continued eating.

The news mentioned that an airplane en route to Alaska from Charlotte crashed somewhere over a field in Colorado earlier that afternoon. The emergency crews sent to handle the disaster never returned. The news anchor said more emergency officials had been sent to investigate, and they would provide more details as they became available.

By the next day, the Denver area had gone dark.

Several more television stations stopped their broadcasting, and the few that remained all had the same message: Evacuate to safe zones west of the Mississippi and avoid the affected areas. A few reported that a forest fire had broken out near Morganton sometime late last night.

Radio stations disappeared, too. Pretty much all of the AM and FM stations went quiet. The especially popular Mama MacDaddy's Mixtape program disappeared. Aside from a few faint signals of warnings to evacuate, it seemed as if everyone had finally decided radio broadcasting wasn't a priority anymore.

Everyone except one.

A conspiracy theorist named Quentin Revere,

who normally broadcast from Nashville but was currently in Los Angeles, seemed to have gotten much more airtime as of late.

"They're not pulling any punches, folks!" Quentin shouted. "They want you out of your homes by any means necessary. They even trotted out the little black girl for the sympathy card. Make no mistake! The global elites are coming for you!"

"I hate that asshole," Rita said, bringing out two hard iced teas and setting them on the card table. She sat down in the rocking chair on one side, opposite Esme who smoked a cigarette and flicked it in the ashtray on the table. Next to the ashtray was the radio. It was late in the evening, and the only sounds were the gentle creaking of their rocking chairs and Quentin Revere screaming about a vampire conspiracy cooked up by the government. There were no sounds of forest life, no animals skittering through trees and leaves in the darkness. Not even crickets.

Esme turned the volume down. "Sorry. It was all I could find that was still on the radio. Everyone else's gone off the air."

"Yeah, I came across him earlier," Rita replied, lighting her own cigarette. "He started usin' a bunch of slurs. I guess he's got nobody left to censor him."

"This one mine?" Esme said, pointing to the iced tea.

"Yeah."

"Thanks, hon."

They drank in silence from their backyard balcony overlooking the mountains. Tonight, the stars dotted the sky like something out of a pleasant dream. One would hardly know that the world was going to hell under a night sky like this.

"I'm sorry about Bella," Esme said.

Rita smiled, then shrugged. "It's okay. I bet she got out. I mean, maybe. Maybe not. Either way, I don't have to invite her to ride it out with us and pretend you're just my housemate."

Esme sipped her tea, lightly chuckling.

"One of the news stations said that more areas near Denver went dark," Rita said. "Lots o' places goin' dark, now. North Carolina, Virginia, South Carolina have all pretty much gone dark. That fire over in Morganton is still goin'. And apparently, they've set up some kind of safe zone out in California. Supposed to be heavily guarded with lots of military. But I don't know what that's supposed to do. Didn't do much good here."

"I guess evacuatin' west would just delay the inevitable," Esme said. "Looks like everywhere's gone to shit."

"Yeah," Rita said in agreement, sipping her tea.

Esme leaned forward, squinting her eyes. "What's that?"

She pointed over the balcony. Something was moving in the trees below.

"Is that a bear?" Esme said, putting her drink down and looking. It was too dark to see for sure. Bears sometimes liked to go for midnight strolls here. There was definitely something moving.

"I'll get the flashlight," Rita said, standing up and

moving back inside. Esme leaned over and squinted.

"Hey, Rita?' Esme called. "Get a gun. And the cross. I don't think that's a bear."

The next morning, Rita and Esme stood over the fire pit, watching the remains of their attacker smolder. Mostly charred ashes now, Esme took the shovel and pulled the blown-out skull out of the flames towards them. There were definitely two sharp fangs protruding from the mouth.

"Fuckin' vampires," Esme said.

It had been a long night.

When the attacker first burst from the trees, he'd let out a hideous scream that Esme afterwards described as sounding "like a banshee outta Hell." He ran extremely fast, and before they could react, he was climbing up the support beams to the balcony. As Rita tried to get a good aim at him, Esme held up the cross. The man leaped onto the railing and snarled, completely unphased by the cross. He readied himself to pounce on Esme. But Rita blasted him in the forehead with a shotgun shell. He fell down from the balcony railing immediately.

As they each came down off the high balcony and approached the body, he didn't seem to be moving. Esme took her spear fashioned from her old hiking stick and jammed it into his chest. Some blood squirted and bubbled out, but he didn't move. She took the cross and placed it on him, expecting it to start burning him or something, but nothing happened.

They debated what to do next.

"Well, the cross doesn't do shit, but the shotgun sure does," Esme said.

"Do we just leave him here?" Rita asked.

"Bury him, maybe?" Esme suggested.

This seemed like a good idea, so they both grabbed a shovel from the wellhouse beside their parked truck and began digging a grave in the center of their backyard. It took them the better part of twenty minutes before they had something remotely close to a grave. Esme suggested they keep digging a bigger pit because it was likely they'd have to put more vampires in it. As she continued digging, she heard Rita let out a shout and fire off another shell.

Jumping, Esme screamed, "What happened?!" She dropped her shovel and ran back to Rita.

"Asshole started twitchin' again!" Rita said, pointing. She'd delivered another shot to the vampire's face, and now it looked virtually unrecognizable as a head apart from the teeth. "It's like he was startin' to get up again."

"Oh God," Esme said. "We shot him in the head and staked his ass! Are those not enough?"

"Well, they seem to keep 'em down for a little bit. But if I didn't know any better, I'd say he was startin' to heal up or somethin'."

"Shotgun to the head hurts 'em, but doesn't kill 'em," Esme said, wondering. "Crosses and stakes don't do anything. There's gotta be a way to kill 'em."

"What if we cut off his head?" Rita asked.

Esme thought for a moment. Then she said, "I'll

be right back. Keep an eye on him."

Esme went inside to grab her shotgun which was already loaded with two shells. Then she went over to the wellhouse and grabbed an axe. When she returned, Rita hadn't moved, and it didn't look like the vampire had either.

"Any movement?" she asked.

"Ain't seen any yet," Rita replied, looking uneasily from the corpse to the dark forest all around them.

Esme took the axe and chopped the vampire's head off. With a crunching sound not unlike chopping cabbage, his head rolled off towards the pit, blood matting the freshly unearthed dirt as it rolled down. Small geysers of blood squirted out of the neck onto the ground.

"Think he's dead?" Rita asked.

"Yeah, I think he's pretty fuckin' dead now," Esme said, looking at the pit. She thought it needed to be deeper. It was possible that more vampires would show up. But what if they were already here?

That sudden thought made her feel vulnerable. They weren't safe standing outside here in the darkness. They needed to get back inside. If one had managed to find them in their remote home, then it was possible more would find them.

She also didn't want a rotting corpse in their backyard.

"Go grab the gasoline and some matches. I'll stand watch." Esme held her gun at the ready, eyeing the dark forest surrounding them as Rita went to the wellhouse where they kept the gasoline for their lawnmower.

Esme didn't trust the darkness. She felt as if there were other vampires out in it, lurking, just waiting for them to lower their guard so they could attack.

When Rita returned with the gasoline and matches, they shoved the decapitated body and kicked its severed head into the pit. Dousing it with gasoline, Esme lit a match and threw it into the pit. The vampire's body immediately caught fire. Flames lit up the pit and cast an eerie luminance onto the dark trees around them.

They took turns through the night keeping watch. No other vampires attacked. Now the sun was coming up, and a few embers and charred bones remained of the motionless corpse.

"Okay, so new plan," Rita said. "Forget the cross and the stakes. Shoot them down. Then chop their fuckin' heads off. Throw 'em in the pit and barbecue their asses."

"Seems like overkill."

"I don't care. As long he's dead."

Now that they knew an effective (if somewhat laborious) method of killing vampires, Esme and Rita spent much of the day resting indoors. There was no way of knowing when or if another vampire would show up, so they decided to rest and reload their guns while they still could.

They didn't encounter anything on Monday or Tuesday. The national news detailed mass traffic jams and evacuation efforts, as well as reports of areas in Colorado, Kansas, Wyoming, Nebraska, Utah, and New Mexico going dark. Troops were deployed to those areas, but they kept going missing. All flights in the country had officially been grounded.

On Wednesday, October 11th, right as they were set to go inside and make dinner, a vampire leaped up onto their backyard balcony. The woman, snarling and drooling blood, startled them both, but Rita was fast. She whipped out the shotgun and blasted the vampire in the face. Blood sprayed out the back of the woman's skull as she fell off the balcony, landing in a crumpled heap twelve feet below. As before, they chopped off her head, threw her in the pit, and set her on fire.

After dinner, they took turns keeping watch through the night. Rita took over for Esme around seven in the morning, and Esme went to get some sleep.

When Esme woke up around noon the next day, she made herself some coffee and turned on the television. Most channels had been reduced to pixelated blurs of static and noise, or what she and Rita called "snow channels." The *PLEASE STANDBY* messages were all gone.

The only remaining station they had played a news cycle of updates. Many parts of Florida had now gone dark. The deployed troops in many areas had gone missing. Much of Colorado and parts of Wyoming and Kansas had gone dark.

The most defeating news came when they

announced that the President, his cabinet, his close officials, and his press secretary had all gone missing sometime the night before.

Pleas to retreat west now stopped, and viewers were advised simply to seek shelter wherever they could. Esme sighed, drank her coffee, and turned the television off.

When Rita woke up around three that afternoon, she discovered Esme standing on the porch with her rifle slung over her shoulder, looking out at the mountainous wilderness around them. The sky looked unusually orange and dim.

"Any news?" Rita asked, coming up beside her.

"The last workin' television station just went out," Esme said. "It's a snow channel, now. President's missin'. Last I heard, they were tellin' everyone to seek shelter wherever."

Rita sighed. "I guess we're really in it now."

"Yeah."

Rita moved closer to Esme and held her hand.

"Never thought we'd be goin' out in style like this."

Esme looked at Rita and chuckled. "The hell you mean? We ain't dead yet. We're defendin' our home from asshole vampires! I'd say that's a pretty badass story."

Rita smiled. Resting her head on Esme's shoulder, she said, "It's really orange out today."

Esme nodded. "I think it's that fire over in Morganton. Guess they weren't able to put it out. It's been burnin' for, what, like a week now?"

"I think so," Rita said. "The whole world has just gone to hell."

Esme smiled. Putting her arm around Rita, she pulled her close and said, "Not yet."

"How many shells you got left?" Rita asked, leaning over the porch railing with her shotgun. Esme, sitting in one of the rocking chairs and reloading the other shotgun, looked at the nearly empty ammunition box on the table next to her.

"Four in the belt, two in the barrels," Esme said, a little winded but still ready to fire off more rounds. She snapped her shotgun closed, ready for the next target.

"Gonna have to switch to the handguns soon," Rita responded, peering intently into the dark woods below.

It was the night of October 13th.

A Friday.

A little before dinnertime, a vampire jumped onto their backyard balcony. As before, they'd dealt with it in short order. Then another jumped onto the balcony. Then another. And another. And soon it appeared that there was a whole herd of vampires moving through the area, and they'd all decided to try their luck with Rita and Esme's cabin. Rita and Esme took care of the vampires one at a time as they'd done with the first few vampires, but the onslaught kept coming too quickly for the two to properly decapitate and immolate them. Once they had a moment to breathe, they set to chopping off heads and moving the bodies to the fire pit (which by now had a steady flame going). However, they would get interrupted by another vampire or two charging out of the dark forest and have to deal with that. So far, they had shot nearly eighty vampires this night.

What started as a distant orange glow the other day had now grown into a vividly yellow horizon against the otherwise black sky. They'd seen enough mountain life in the cabin to know it was the forest fire. But it had to be a monstrously large fire to span that far across the horizon.

"Shit, got another one!" Rita yelled, aiming her gun at the far end of the balcony. A woman had climbed up on the side of the railing, snarling and gnashing her teeth. Before she could charge over at them, Rita fired a shell into the woman's head, splitting it open. Blood splattered onto the support beam behind her as her body fell lifeless to the ground below, joining about thirty other dead bodies.

"Jesus Christ," Rita said as she readied her last shell. "That smell!" The stench from the bloody corpses was overpowering. There hadn't been a chance to dispose of the bodies all evening, but both of them knew they needed to take care of it fast. Otherwise, the vampires would heal and start attacking again.

Esme stood up from her chair with her shotgun ready just in time to see another vampire climb over the balcony railing to her left and charge.

She was ready, though.

"*Eat some, bitch!*" she shouted, shooting the man in his abdomen. This made him fall over, but he kept scrambling towards her. Before she could aim at his head, he pounced on her, knocked the barrel aside, and pinned her down. His eyes glowed white and radiated malice. He opened his mouth wide, revealing his bloodstained mouth. His breath was hot, and bloody scraps of flesh hung in-between his teeth.

"Rita!" she screamed, trying desperately to push him off of her.

Before the man could bite Esme, Rita shot him in the head. His brains splattered onto the balcony, and some blood sprayed onto Esme's shirt. His body went limp, and Esme pushed him off of her. Rita helped her up. Esme grabbed a nearby rag from her rocking chair and wiped the blood from her shirt.

"I'm switchin' to the rifle. Outta shells," Rita said, going over to the card table where her rifle and box of cartridges were.

"We need a goddamn break," Esme said, shaking as she tossed aside the rag and moved towards her shotgun. "Gotta burn these bodies."

Rita looked at the corpse. Even with his head splayed open like a gory catastrophe, his twitching body still seemed like it could leap up and take her.

"Yeah, you're right. We got like thirty bodies down there. I'll chop the heads off if you cover me." With that, Rita slung her rifle over her shoulder and pocketed one of the handguns. She moved to pick up the bloodstained axe lying against the wall.

"Help me get this body off the porch, first," Esme

said.

Rita grabbed the still-twitching vampire's arms as Esme grabbed the legs, and together they heaved him over the railing. He landed amongst the other corpses with a dull thud.

"Fuck vampires," Rita said.

"Fuck 'em to hell," Esme replied.

It was no use.

Rita managed to decapitate all of the bodies, but before they could throw even half of them in the fire pit, another onslaught of vampires came charging out of the forest.

"Fuck!" Esme shouted, blasting away as quickly as she could. She and Rita backed up to the balcony stairwell. Rita grabbed her rifle and joined in with the shooting. Every time one vampire went down, another took its place. They continued shooting as they climbed the stairs back to the balcony.

Rita and Esme had hunted enough deer and turkey over the years to be good with moving targets. That wasn't the problem. The problem was that there were too many targets now.

"Shit. I'm out of shells," Esme said.

"Hang on!" Rita said, shooting a vampire in the face with her rifle. It fell over the balcony and landed with the rest of the bodies.

Esme darted inside to grab her rifle and the handguns. During a brief lull, Rita quickly reloaded her rifle with cartridges from the card table. She closed the chamber just as two more vampires leaped onto the porch. She managed to shoot one, then the other, in the head. They both went down.

We've gotta burn the bodies, she thought. *There's too many of them now.*

Two more vampires emerged from the forest, howling like demonic wolves.

Rita couldn't stop to think now, shoving more cartridges in. After reloading, she leaned over the balcony railing and took the vampires out one at a time. More kept coming. Every time she took one down, another emerged from the forest to take his place.

"Where the fuck they comin' from?!" she yelled as she took down two more. Sweat dripped off her brow. She started to feel a gnawing sense of panic as she quickly reloaded her cartridges for the third time in less than two minutes.

She could see their white, glowing eyes amidst the trees. There must have been dozens of them lying in wait just beyond the edge of the forest. They glowed, then vanished, then reappeared elsewhere. It was like watching dozens of fireflies flitter about in the darkness.

Without warning, two more charged. Almost like an automaton triggered to react at an exact moment, Rita put a bullet between both of their heads.

Then another one walked out. But this one wasn't running or even charging the cabin anymore. He simply walked towards her, teeth bared. He was also smiling, like he knew something she didn't. This unnerved Rita.

Fucker thinks this is funny?

She shot him in the face. As he went down, more eyes flickered beyond the edge of the trees.

They're movin' around out there.

She reloaded her gun, then readied it, unsure which direction they'd come from next.

Two on her left.

With matching speed, she blew one's head off. The other tried to run in a wide arc away from the gun, but she anticipated something like this.

"Fuck you, asshole!" she said, shooting him in the head. He went down like the other one. Another one walked from the forest to her left, smiling. She shot this one, too. Reloaded the cartridges. Two more on her left, then on her right. Each time, she made sure her bullets found their mark.

The eyes continued to shift in the darkness of the trees after each shot. Then the process would repeat. It was almost getting monotonous to her now.

It finally dawned on her what was happening.

They're makin' me waste ammunition! They want me to keep shootin' at 'em!

The idea horrified her. Up until this moment, she'd thought they were just ravenous, vicious creatures of the night. She thought they were once people like her and Esme, but that part of them had been lost to this demonic nature. Now, she realized with growing dread, it was fairly obvious that they could think lucid thoughts.

Plan attacks.

They can coordinate with each other!

"I ain't goin' down like this!" Rita shouted, continuing to fire away. Each time her rifle ran out of cartridges, she quickly reloaded. Some of the vampires took the opportunity to charge at the balcony with ferocious speed, but Rita was faster. No vampire could make it to the balcony without a bullet to the face.

How much longer can we keep this up?

"Esme!" Rita yelled. "Tell me you've got a gun!"

"Hang on, I'm comin'!" Esme said, coming out with a tray. On it were the handguns and leftover boxes of bullets. Quickly setting it on the balcony table, she grabbed a handgun and joined in with the shooting.

The sun came up when the onslaught ended. At first, they didn't even realize the sun had come up because the glow of the forest fire hadn't left. But once it appeared that no more vampires would be coming out, they realized they had been at it all night.

Esme rested against the balcony railing, but Rita pulled her towards the stairwell leading to the backyard.

"Come on. We've got to deal with the bodies."

Exhausted and bordering on delirious, Esme grabbed the axe. Rita grabbed the shovel, and together they started decapitating the remaining bodies.

Some two hundred bodies lay strewn over their backyard, clumped over each other like a grisly crime scene. The tomato garden was now buried and crushed under the corpses of several vampires. Together, Rita and Esme chopped off the heads.

Whenever one started to stir, they took their handguns and shot it in the head again, then quickly chopped off its head.

They realized that maybe they didn't have to burn the corpses just yet. After all, the ones they'd decapitated the night before hadn't gotten back up. They certainly hadn't sprouted new heads in place of their old ones.

"I guess choppin' off their heads is enough," Esme said.

"Enough to do the trick, sure," Rita said, driving the blade of her shovel deep into the neck of an old woman vampire. Her head went flying down the hill back towards the forest. "But we'll need to burn them eventually. Too many dead bodies. Rottin' and smellin' corpses and shit. And I, for one, look forward to settin' these fuckers on fire."

Once they finished decapitating the bodies, they went back to the porch and took stock of what ammunition they had left. They'd used up all the cartridges and bullets in the boxes. There were no more shotgun shells or rifle rounds. Now they just had four handguns left, each fully loaded with eight rounds, and the spears fashioned from their walking sticks.

Esme leaned on the table, catching her breath. Then she looked at Rita. "We ain't gonna last another night of this."

Rita shook her head. "Those fuckers drained us. They played the numbers game with us. They *knew* to drain our ammo. Now we're fucked."

138

"We still have the spears," Esme said. "And the axe and shovel."

Even as she spoke, Esme realized how useless those would be in the event of an onslaught. She looked out at the mountains again. As the sun rose, thick smoke from the great fire filled the sky. Their peaceful paradise had been dragged down to hell with the rest of the world, and now the fires were closing in on them. The home they'd built together was going to burn one way or another.

Rita put her hand on Esme's shoulder. "Look, we've made as good a run as we can. Maybe we hop in the truck and head west?"

Esme shook her head. "There's nowhere left to go these things can't get to. We'd just be livin' on the run until the inevitable happens."

Rita dropped her gun and hugged Esme. "I'm so sorry, Esme. I'm so sorry."

Esme pushed her back, grabbed her face, and said, "You listen to me. This is our home. We're gonna ride it out together. Yes, we're gonna die. Pretty sure of that now. But at least we'll be together and in our home. Got it?"

Rita nodded, wiping the tears from her eyes. "You sure about this?"

Esme smiled, ignoring her own tears. "Goin' out with you, guns blazin' and vampire heads explodin'? Fuck yeah."

The next onslaught happened that night.

As before, hordes of vampires emerged from the

forest slowly. Methodically. The onslaught wasn't as large this time. Only about twenty vampires or so. When they took out the last of these vampires, Esme looked at Rita. "How many bullets you got left?" she asked.

"Five, I think," Rita said.

"I got this handgun. That's it. Last one. Only used one round so far."

They grabbed a shovel and the axe and walked down the porch steps to the ground below. Without hesitation Esme took the axe and drove the blade hard against the nearest body at the neck. She was so tired that it took her three jabs before the head finally severed. They hadn't had time to immolate any of the bodies from the previous night's attack, so they didn't bother with dragging any bodies to the fire pit now. Exhausted, sleep-deprived, and too tired for conversation, they moved to chop the heads off in silence.

As Esme approached a body near the forest, she looked up and realized it was too late. There were some thirty or forty pairs of glowing eyes standing in the woods, just watching her. As her eyes adjusted to the darkness, she could see the vampires smiling devilish grins. She dropped her axe to the ground, staring right back. They'd won, and they knew that she knew this.

"Rita," Esme called over, "I love you."

"Shut the fuck up!" Rita said, throwing her shovel at the vampires and grabbing Esme by the wrist, leading her back to the cabin. She eyed the vampires in the forest as they each took slow steps towards them. "Come on, we're gettin' outta here. Pick up your axe!"

Rita intended to hop in the truck and haul ass out of there. But once they reached the porch, she saw many vampires gathered there like a cultish assembly, blocking them from the truck. There were vampires on the roof of the cabin. There were vampires on the porch, blocking them from the walking sticks they'd fashioned into spears. There were vampires in the trees, perfectly poised to jump on them. Esme swung the axe, warning the vampires to stay away, but the creatures marched onward. Finally, she tossed it at the vampires. The axe blade sank into the chest of a woman, but she seemed unphased and kept slinking forward.

Rita threw open the front door and led Esme to the kitchen. Here they saw that several vampires had broken in through the windows upstairs and were now climbing over the railing, climbing down the walls like spiders.

"Get the hell outta our cabin, you fuck-faces!" Rita spent her last four rounds on the intruders. Esme also joined in and took out four of the vampires.

Now they were completely out of bullets.

The vampires outside began to move in like a slow funeral procession, except they were each licking their lips and baring their fangs, ready to drink the blood of these two women who had fought them off so ferociously.

Rita and Esme threw their guns at the vampires

and moved closer together, crouching down on the kitchen floor near the sink.

"Well, it was a hell of a ride," Rita said, grabbing a knife from the countertop.

"I'm glad we're goin' out together," Esme said, burying her face in Rita's shoulder.

Rita aimed the knife at the approaching vampires. As the creatures closed in, Rita and Esme held each other close.

THE SHEPHERD

Quentin Revere walked into the small, black-walled studio and took his seat. His chair squeaked as he got situated. The studio clock read 5:25:05, the seconds ticking away without a concern for the chaos unfolding in the rest of the world. The room smelled of cigar smoke, but Quentin wouldn't want it any other way. This was his playground, and it was almost time for another broadcast. He picked up his show notes and looked over them once more.

"Bradley," he called to a blonde man sitting over by the tapes. The blonde man looked up from what he was writing on a legal pad.

"Boss?" Bradley said.

"Did you cut those quotes from the girl's interview yet?"

"Yeah, I got them cued and everything. I also got the one about California."

"Good. Good," Quentin said, grabbing a highlighter and marking the section labeled *Naomi Perry* in his notes. He highlighted a few more quotes from the speech.

That'll be good, he thought.

The clock now read 5:27. He started his vocal warm-ups. As he trilled his lips and hummed through his vowel sounds, he glanced over at Brenda near the opposite end of the room. Brenda was already on the phone screening callers.

"It's about time, boss. You ready?" Kyle called from his computer station opposite Bradley.

"Like a fox," Quentin said, deciding not to call out his broadcast technician for the Alabama hat adorning his balding head. Even though the game against Tennessee was in just a few days, Quentin had a much more pressing issue on his mind. He was ready to reach through his microphone, come through the radio speakers, and grab listeners by their shirt collars as he had done for close to five years now.

5:29 PM.

He grabbed his headphones, slipped them comfortably over his ears, and pulled the overhead microphone close to his mouth.

As soon as the clock turned 5:30:00, Kyle pushed a button on his computer. The hard-rock guitar riff introducing *The Revere Zone with Quentin Revere* began, complete with sound bites from action movies, embarrassing quotes from politicians caught on tape, and snippets of fans cheering his name. At the end of the intro came his famous catchphrase, "You're cornered, and I got ya, ya lyin' sack o' crap!" This was followed by a woman (Brenda from her intern days) declaring to the listener, "Prepare to cry, pinko commies. You're listening to *The Revere Zone with Quentin Revere.*"

As the theme song drew to a close, Quentin

leaned towards his microphone.

"Folks, it is Friday, October 6th," he growled, hardly taking a breath before moving on to the next sentence. "We've got a big, uh, big show for you today. Lots to cover. But the first thing we're gonna talk about . . . the first thing . . . really, it's the biggest thing, which is why I'm starting the show with it. So don't miss this. This is really important, folks. I went over this yesterday, and it's really too big not to repeat, so this is for everyone who missed it yesterday. Listen to me, and do not forget this! You listening to me? Good! Do not miss this!"

He leaned even closer to his microphone and screamed, "*There! Are! No! Vampires!*"

It was pushing on to dinner time now. Harry Graham had set out that morning from Okemah and figured he could probably hit Knoxville by nightfall, then Fayetteville by Saturday afternoon, just in time for his sister's wedding. Quentin Revere's radio broadcast was keeping him awake.

"And you say, 'But Quentin! I *saw* the videos of those vampires attacking people on the news! The liberal media wouldn't *lie* to me!' If you believe that, folks, I mean, if you honestly believe that, then I've got just two words for you: *You! Are! A! Sucker!* You are a sucker and a gullible little sheep! *Baa! Baa! Baa!* You actually believe the liberal media wouldn't lie to you? You actually believe they wouldn't make up something as Satanic and vile as vampires?!"

Lucinda was marrying some accountant-type

from North Carolina. Harry had met him only once at the family Christmas party last year and thought the man was a real limp-dick. The man's hands were so soft when he shook them that Harry wondered if the man had ever even heard of the phrase "manual labor" before. He didn't say anything to Lucinda, though. If she was happy, he was happy. An accountant would be good with money, too, so he shrugged it off.

When Harry first heard the reports about the disappearances, he called Lucinda to see what the plan was. When he'd spoken to her on Wednesday, she said she'd heard the reports but hadn't seen anything. It wasn't until Thursday, when Quentin Revere started calling the whole thing a scam, that Harry decided to go ahead with the trip. He called and left Lucinda a message saying he was coming.

He didn't think much of Lucinda not answering and assumed that she'd merely been away from the phone, probably mired in wedding preparations. *If it really were all that bad, Lucinda would have called back*, he decided.

Harry had been staring at endless fields of flat farmland and trailer parks for too long now, and he needed the radio to keep him awake. He reached into the cooler sitting passenger for another soda-pop. Snapping the tab open, he slurped the good stuff and let out a satisfying exhale.

"That's some good shit right there, I tell you what, Jessie," he said to his truck, setting the soda-pop in the drink holder and patting the dashboard enthusiastically.

Jessie was brand new when he got her back in April. She came with a built-in CD player and a nice sound system. Truthfully, he preferred the radio to CDs, but it was nice to have the option.

"You know something, Jess? I think we'll find a nice little hotel somewhere near Knoxville, get a good night's rest, and hit it early tomorrow morning."

Looking down at the radio, he saw the clock read 5:46.

"Look," Quentin said earnestly through the radio speakers. "I've been covering the truth for almost five years now. On-air. You all know I report the truth they don't want you to know. I started as a kid working with my dad in west Tennessee before I got my own show, uh, you know, warning you all about the New World Order and their plans for world domination and how they put the brainwashing chemicals into the very water you drink to keep you dumb and loyal to the government authorities."

Harry nodded along, patting his cooler. "That's why I got my soda-pops, thankee very much."

"Now we've all heard about this so-called 'vampire outbreak' that's been going on over in North Carolina. We got reports of things happening in South Carolina now. And Virginia. Now think about this, folks. What is that? That's the southeast, folks."

There was a dramatic pause here.

"I said before the break that I'd expose the New World Order's plan with this, so I want you to think about this. This thing . . . they're calling it a vampire outbreak. It starts in North Carolina, right? Then it allegedly—because vampires aren't real, in case you're a moron—moves into South Carolina. And Virginia. And I predict they'll be saying it's in Tennessee next. Well, I broadcast from Nashville, folks. Then Georgia and Florida next. Then Arkansas. Then Alabama. Wanna know how I know? Well, think about it! What do those states all have in common? That's right, folks. They're all in the Bible belt. They are targeting Christians, folks."

Harry shook his head. Looking to his left, he realized that there were an awful lot of vehicles in the lanes heading west, or what his dad would've called a "pig's shitload" of cars and trucks. He'd noticed a lot of traffic, but now it looked as if they were coming to a serious traffic jam over there. The cars were barely moving.

Harry whistled. "Look at all them sheeps, Jessie. Buncha stupid dumbasses just throwin' their lives away for a government lie."

He had the entire road practically to himself heading east on I-40. He realized he hadn't seen another car on his side of the road in probably about two or three hours.

Harry took another swig of his soda-pop, this time spilling some on his brown beard.

"Ah shit," he said, wiping his hand off on his beard and then on the seat next to him. "Sorry, Jess," he said. "Shoulda brought some damn napkins."

"And once again, I have to be the shepherd of truth," Quentin Revere grumbled through the radio.

"It is my mission to wake as many people up to God's truth as I can. Look, folks, I'm just calling it like I see it. They're coming for the Christians! For God's people!"

Harry drove on.

By the time Harry pulled into a hotel parking lot outside of Knoxville, it was dark outside. Harry thought it was oddly quiet as there were no cars on the road at all here. In fact, the entire area looked deserted. Nearby buildings were completely shrouded in darkness. Harry parked the red truck and got out. The cool night air made him throw on his red jacket. Then he went inside.

The hotel lights were on, but nobody stood at the desk. He went up to the desk, rang the bell, and waited. Looking around, it all looked clean, but he noticed that the trashcan was overflowing. *Someone should get on that*, he thought.

He rang the bell again.

After another minute, he rang again.

Where the hell are they?

He was dog-tired and getting impatient. Leaning over the counter, he tried to peer into the back office. He didn't see anyone back there. "Hello!" he called out, but there was no response. He went behind the counter and looked into the office, but he didn't see anyone in there.

Maybe the bathroom?

Coming back around the front desk he moved towards the bathroom. Going in, he called out again,

"Anyone here? I need a room." Again, there was just silence. Shrugging his shoulders, he decided to go pee since he was in the bathroom anyway. Once he finished, he went back out to the lobby and waited at the desk again. He rang the bell once more.

"I'm not ringing this bell for shits and giggles, people," he called out. There was a slight echo of his voice and nothing else.

It started to hit him just how quiet it all was. There was no outside traffic. The lobby television was off. He started to wonder if he was the only person here. Then he noticed a piece of paper taped to the top of the counter. It read:

Left on 10/5, heading west.
Keys are under desk; take what you need;
Be safe; God bless.
- Dave

Harry stared, dumbfounded.

"Are they for real?" He moved behind the desk and found a basket tray full of keys in envelopes with the room numbers on them. He picked up one that read 151. He looked around.

"So, I'm just allowed to take a key and have a free hotel room?" he called out to no one in particular.

Nobody answered.

He looked down at the envelope again. *Maybe there's an upside to this hoax after all*, he thought.

"Okay, I'm just gonna take a key and help myself to a room, then," he said out loud. "If I'm doing it wrong, just let me know, and I'll pay up."

Coming back around the desk, he went outside to his truck. Reaching inside, he grabbed his luggage and shut the door. The quiet was unnerving. He should've been able to hear a distant car running, a dog barking, someone playing music for money. Something. But all he heard was a low wind blowing leaves, and that was it.

And without the parking lot lights, it was very dark. He could barely make out the white letters that spelled J-E-S-S-I-E on his truck's rear window.

Going back inside, he was surprised to see a man and a woman, probably a little older than him, walking through the lobby towards him. All three stopped, shocked to see each other. The bald man had a faded denim jacket and blue jeans while his brunette wife wore a reddish-brown corduroy jacket and black jeans. Harry thought they both looked like hell. Her hair was disheveled, his face was covered in ash, and both looked like they hadn't slept in years.

"Hey! Is anybody running this place?" Harry asked.

The man shook his head. Pointing to the sign on the counter, he said in a distraught voice, "No, everyone's left. We're leaving, too. You leaving?"

Harry shook his head. "I just got in from Okemah."

"You should get out. It's not safe here."

Harry cocked his head to the side, skeptical. *Another little sheep. Scared of the big bad wolf and flocking right to the big bad wolf's den.* "Where you from?" Harry asked, not wanting to be confrontational.

"Greensboro," the man said. "Listen, my wife and I are headed out. We stopped to rest for a while, but we're gonna head on. It's not safe here. You should head out, too."

Harry laughed. "Jeez, you fell for the hoax, huh?"

"What?" the man said, looking at him quizzically.

His wife tugged on his arm. "Come on, let's go."

Harry pointed outside. "I came from Oklahoma, and I saw the entire I-40 blocked up with people trying to get out. But you know it's not real. The vampires."

"What?" The man suddenly looked very angry.

"Isaac, let's go," the woman protested.

"It's not real," Harry repeated, giving them an apologetic look. "It's just a government conspiracy to evict you from your homes and target Christianity."

Isaac looked ready to punch Harry, but his wife tugged on his arm, moving him towards the exit.

"Tell that to my son, asshole," the man spat.

"Isaac, let's go," the woman said, tears visible on her face now.

"You know what? Go ahead and stay," Isaac spat. "I hope you wake up with your throat ripped out, you piece of shit!" The man and his wife left the building. Harry rolled his eyes and marched onwards with the keys to room 151.

Some people just don't know what good manners are anymore, he thought sadly.

Getting to the room and thoroughly exhausted, Harry plopped down on the bed and tossed his bags onto a chair. He turned the TV on. Many of the channels, particularly the local news stations, were off-air with the static multi-colored *PLEASE STAND BY DUE TO TECHNICAL DIFFICULTIES* screen displaying. The cable networks were still on, but most of them were just running news of the vampire hoax. There was more footage of vampires prowling around like weirdos in the streets. Harry wouldn't be fooled by any of it. Quentin had explained how it was all staged by Hollywood actors and makeup effects people. None of it was real.

He'd make it to Fayetteville tomorrow. He decided it'd be good to give Lucinda a ring. Picking up the phone, he punched in the long-distance toll number, then Lucinda's number. If there was nobody here to charge him, he might as well make a long-distance call.

He was instantly greeted with a recording stating, "All calls are busy. Please try again later." He looked at the phone, annoyed, then hung up. Laying back in bed, he stared at the ceiling.

All these idiots just up and abandoned their homes because the government told them to. Now there's nobody to run the phone companies.

He showered next. As he showered, he started thinking about the more worrisome implications of people just leaving.

Well, shit. If there's nobody there, then who's gonna run the nuclear power plants? Or the military bases with weapons? I hope they at least shut those things down before they left. Harry didn't have a clue how nuclear plants operated, but he did know they could explode like Chernobyl or meltdown like Three Mile Island.

Crawling into bed, his mind began to fixate on

other horrible things that might happen in the absence of people. *There might not be any cops to keep the streets safe. Crime'll go up. Looting, thefts, carjackings. Hell, anyone sticking around will be free to do whatever they want. Jeez, I wonder if they have any nukes just lying around in these places.*

The last thought Harry had before drifting off to sleep was, *It won't be vampires that kill us all. It'll be other people.*

Harry got a good night's rest. No one had left much food out for breakfast, but there were some leftover oranges and bagels in the lobby. He grabbed a few of each, hopped back in the truck with his clothes, started Jessie up, and hit the road again.

The sky was relatively clear, and aside from the occasional car heading west, Harry didn't see anyone else on the road.

It seemed as though most of the local news affiliates had gone out, which was fine with Harry. Quentin Revere seemed to have gained even more airtime as a result. Harry turned up the dial and started listening.

". . . don't know if you saw this, but they started a giant forest fire over in North Carolina last night. Somewhere in North Carolina. Matter of fact, I can now confirm that independent reporters who have stayed behind have in fact seen men dressed in black suits breaking and entering into homes and taking out religious artifacts. Bibles, crosses, pictures of Jesus, you name it. They don't want anyone to have access to the Bible! They are trying to eradicate any history of Jesus in America."

Harry laughed. "Wow! They didn't waste any time, did they, Jess?"

The truck hummed along the road.

"Folks, I know we're tuning in a lot earlier than usual. Turns out Kyle, our broadcast technician, is just as gullible as anyone. He's a little fruitcake. He took off yesterday, and, uh, we've had to scramble. But look at it this way, folks! He was scared! Like so many innocent, otherwise well-meaning Christians are right now. They're scared! The government knows this. The government planned this with New World Order operatives. Their mission is twofold, you see. The first step is to get the Christians out of their homes. That way the government can go in and destroy their Bibles, destroy their churches when they're not looking. The second step is to get everyone to California. Because of course everyone's gonna need help getting resituated. But do you think for one minute that that help is gonna come without strings attached?" Quentin laughed hysterically, then growled, "You're an idiot if you think that!"

Harry heard something that sounded like a really loud leaf blower outside. He looked out his window, but there were no other cars on the road, not even on the other side.

What the hell is that sound? he wondered.

"Vampires aren't real!" Quentin started screaming. "I can't even believe I have to say that! I mean, how dumb does the New World Order think we are? Vampires! Seriously? Vampires? Of all the

155

things they could have chosen—terrorists, disease, nuclear invasion, alien invaders, uh, um, sentient shark people disguised like humans—they go with vampires! Vampires aren't real! They actually expect us to believe that Dracula is running around creating more of him! It's just idiotic, folks!"

The sound hadn't gone away, so Harry rolled his window down. Now he could hear it very clearly: a tornado siren was going off.

It wailed throughout the mountainous region like a dying cat wailing its last breaths. But even after a few minutes, it hadn't stopped. Harry leaned forward to look out at the sky. On any side of him and Jessie, the sky looked pretty clear. There was not a single cloud to be seen.

Why the siren? he wondered.

"Folks, if anyone is listening to this broadcast, do yourself a favor! Go back home! Don't let the government scare you out of your homes! It's all nonsense! Remember, they want to take your rights away! Don't let them!"

Harry had a sudden thought. *What if they're about to nuke the area?*

He looked for any planes in the sky ready to drop a bomb on him, but he didn't see any.

He remembered Quentin saying something yesterday about the President saying he wouldn't use nuclear bombs. He continued to wonder why the tornado siren was going off, and why it hadn't stopped after five minutes of constant wailing. Grim images appeared in his mind of a blinding flash over the mountain peaks followed by a sudden blast of fire

156

engulfing the trees and road all around him, incinerating him and Jessie instantly. The very idea made him shudder uncomfortably. There'd be no one around to help him, and no one else to partake in such a hellish demise.

Then a thought came to him.

"Of course," Harry finally said out loud. "The siren's probably broken because there's no one here to turn it off. See what I mean, Jessie? People done up and left, and now stuff's going to shit."

It didn't matter. What mattered was that in a little while, he'd be at Lucinda's wedding. After the ceremony, there'd be a family gathering for photos and the reception party. He'd have a few beers, share a few laughs, argue over which football team was the best, and hit the road for home tomorrow. Less people here just meant less traffic to deal with.

"There are no vampires here, folks! It's just a mind game! *Don't fall for it!*"

Harry grabbed another soda-pop from the cooler. He flipped the tab open and slurped a huge gulp. "Yes, ma'am, I think we're gonna be A-OK, Jessie."

The tornado sirens hadn't stopped wailing as he passed an exit sign pointing towards Asheville.

THE FLOCK

October 6

Harry Graham wasn't the only one listening to Quentin Revere's program.

In Bracey, Virginia, Bertie Zuckerman hit rewind on the VCR. Whoever rented the tape last from the video store hadn't rewound it. It was a movie about some family crossing paths with dangerous criminals on a river rafting adventure. He'd rented the movie last Friday but ended up so busy that he wasn't able to watch it before it was due to be returned. In fact, he'd meant to see it when it had been out in theaters, but the cases he'd been working on at that time prevented him from doing so. When he wasn't working cases at the office, he was working them at home.

He couldn't remember the last time he'd been able to just loaf around and play hooky all day. Time was money, as the old saying went. But when everyone else at the firm decided to flee west on Thursday morning (including all the judges and seemingly everyone else in town), Bertie stayed behind. He'd taken the tape back only to discover the video store had been abandoned. Figuring he wouldn't be incurring a late fee for his video rental

158

just yet, he took it back home with a promise to himself that he was going to watch the damn movie this time.

As the tape rewound, Bertie went to his model tramp steamer over on the kitchen table. The connected pieces were dry enough now that he could continue working on the smokestack section. Sitting down in a chair, he began snapping the unused parts out of their kits.

God, when was the last time I built a model? High school?

Pancake, his pet calico cat, bounded down the stairs and into the kitchen, rubbing up against his leg and meowing.

"Hey, Pancake. You want some lettuce, little guy?" Bertie said, leaning to scratch under Pancake's chin. Pancake purred and gave him a sideways glance that indicated his desire for lettuce. Setting his model pieces back on the table, Bertie got up and headed towards the fridge.

He flipped the kitchen radio on as he pulled open the refrigerator, scanning the shelves for the bag of lettuce. With everyone gone and nobody there to maintain order, he knew it was important to stay informed.

Behind him, he could hear Quentin Revere on the radio.

". . . you know, the video with the, uh, the man biting down on the woman and screaming and looks like it was filmed out of someone's bathroom? That one. Then there's the one with all those bodies just lying around. It's the one out of Wilmington, where the bodies start getting back up. Point is, we've all seen the videos, okay?"

Closing the fridge, Bertie went over and gave Pancake a leaf of lettuce. Pancake took the lettuce in his mouth and darted off with it towards the living room. Bertie chuckled as he sat back down at the kitchen table and resumed tinkering with the model tramp steamer.

"I can now confirm," Quentin said emphatically from the radio, "that all these videos we're seeing are staged fakes. I have in my hand papers from a high-ranking official in the government saying on record that the US government did in fact hire Hollywood producers and actors—and I guess makeup people and special effects people since it's Hollywood and blood effects and stuff—to create public propaganda videos to incite fear in the citizenry into surrendering their rights. Into leaving their homes. It's the moon landing all over again, folks. Isn't that just unbelievable? That is simply incredible, but that's our government for you."

Bertie laughed. He figured his partners would all come back feeling pretty embarrassed for letting the hoax dupe them. In the meantime, he would enjoy the quiet solitude of his home with some overdue fun time.

In the living room, the VCR clicked. The tape had finished rewinding. Bertie got up, turned the radio off, moved his model pieces to the living room table, and hit play on the VCR.

*

October 6

Over in Lincolnton, North Carolina, Marsha Waterstone turned off the lights to *MARSHA'S ANTIQUES AND ODDITIES*, locked up the front door, and walked to her car. The sun had disappeared behind the trees lining the road, and the gravel parking lot was empty except for her white roadster.

When she climbed in and turned a key in the ignition, the car roared to life. It was the only sound other than the wind that could be heard. The absence of crickets chirping or dogs barking in the distance was unsettling.

She'd considered going home earlier but held out hope that someone was still around to shop. Unfortunately, she only had one person visit the store that day, and he only popped in to tell her to evacuate. He didn't buy anything before he left, and no one else showed up all day. Now, her car and the wind were the only sounds keeping her company.

I guess I'll have to evacuate, too, she thought miserably. Driving away, she turned on the radio. The news had only gotten worse since she last tuned in that morning.

". . . and the Raleigh battalion has gone missing," the reporter said. "This is coming at a time when many local news affiliates in North Carolina have ceased their broadcasting. Increasingly, media officials are calling this 'going dark.' In other words, a place has gone dark once no more news comes from that area."

"Lord Almighty," Marsha said. "They're just not going to do anything about it, are they?" She mentally kicked herself. *I should have left yesterday. This is real. The Antichrist is nigh, and this is the horseman of death.*

She hadn't wanted to believe it was vampires at first. That was too ridiculous, the stuff of children's fantasy. But then she'd seen the videos. And then she saw the Naomi Perry interview. And then areas started going dark. She'd been hopeful that the battalion in Raleigh would be able to take care of the situation, and she wouldn't have to go anywhere. After all, Raleigh was about three hours west of her. How quickly could this thing actually spread?

She'd felt confident enough to open her store today, but after only one customer who couldn't even count as a lookie-loo and now this report of the battalion going missing, she felt that evacuating was unavoidable.

When she pulled into her driveway, the reporter gave an update on missing North Carolinians. "The last numbers we had coming out were well over eight thousand missing. In fact, we had it at 963 missing just out of Winston-Salem alone at last report. And more videos of these attacks have come to light. We can now confirm that the so-called vampires have overrun Winston-Salem. The new estimates are over four-thousand missing. That is just in the Winston-Salem area alone. Actual numbers for the state are much, much higher and changing every minute. And we remind our audiences these are numbers reported as missing to state and local authorities. They are not counting known evacuees as among the numbered."

Marsha parked her car and turned it off. The radio went silent, and now she was left with her raw, nervous dread.

I should've left. I should've left. The horseman of death is going to kill me.

Once inside, she turned on her small kitchen radio, poured some food and water for Delilah, and broke out two eggs for dinner. Filling up a pot with water to boil them in, she heard the reporter say, "Earlier, we reported 43 people missing in the Charlotte area. That number has since risen. According to the sheriff's office, there are now a staggering 677 people who are unaccounted for."

Marsha paused. Winston-Salem was already too close for comfort, but Charlotte was only about forty minutes southeast of her. Much closer. As she put the eggs in the pot, fear gripped her. She wondered if she should even bother with making dinner. Should she just pack up a few things, grab Delilah, and head out now? Or wait until morning?

Where am I supposed to go?

As if the reporter somehow read Marsha's mind, he said, "Again, if you are in the affected areas, drop what you are doing and get out now. Get your family out. Do not pack anything. Evacuate as far west as you can, preferably at least past the Mississippi River. Do not seek any previous safe zones in your area as they are no longer safe."

I'm gonna have to leave my home. I'm gonna have to evacuate. I don't want to turn into a vampire. I don't want to be torn apart like that guy on the news.

The images of the man's head being torn off as several vampires dragged his body into a ditch would be forever burned into her memory. She didn't want to think about it happening to her.

Maybe it won't happen to me. Maybe they'll take care of it before it reaches here.

She went over to the radio and began turning the dial.

"Anyone missing near me?" she asked aloud to no one in particular, worried that it was already too late for her and the other people of Lincolnton.

Most of the usual programs only returned hissing static. She switched to the AM band. What few programs she found either played commercials or more reports of missing people. One mentioned a fire breaking out in Morganton, which was about forty minutes northwest of her. Moments later, the same broadcast mentioned several people missing near Morganton, which meant that she was officially in the midst of the areas "going dark."

The world is ending, she thought. She felt her heart beat faster. She almost thought she could hear the horseman galloping down the road, coming for her.

Hoping against hope for some easier solution than abandoning her home, she turned the dial and found a man screaming at the top of his lungs. "This is all a fake, staged operation!" he shouted. "It's designed to uproot the good Christians of this country out of their homes! There are no vampires! Stay in your homes! Do not let the government scare you into leaving your homes! There are no vampires! You can sleep soundly in your own beds, folks! It's all made up!"

What's this?

Marsha listened to the man yell, surprised by how gruff and different he sounded from virtually everyone else on the radio. The man spoke with such intensity and speed that she wondered if he ever stopped to take a breath.

"Think about this, folks! We've all seen the videos. But really, that's the only evidence we have of it. You haven't actually seen a vampire yourself, have you? Of course not! And that's the game, folks. They get the Hollywood liberals to help make these videos with actors and special effects crews to help the government create this phony-baloney crisis so they can kick all the Christians out of the Bible-belt," he growled.

The more she listened, the more her nerves relaxed. A sense of calm washed over her like a rejuvenating rain. There was no horseman down the road.

I mean, of course. Vampires aren't real. It's as plain as day. God, I feel like an idiot. Getting all worked up over nothing. It's just 'The War of the Worlds' broadcast all over again. Hysteria. Nothing more.

"There are no missing people, folks," the man said. "We're going to take a break. When we come back, we're gonna look closer at how Hollywood helped the government fake this crisis. *The Revere Zone with Quentin Revere* will be right back, folks."

Marsha's golden retriever Delilah walked into the room right as the radio commercials began. Marsha looked at Delilah, petted her on the head, and said,

"Well, old girl, looks like we won't have to go anywhere after all. God is good. And man, as usual, is dumb."

October 7

In Easley, South Carolina, Sara and Mason Hendrickson were at their kitchen table. It was around noon. They sat hunched over elementary-aged educational books, some legal notepads, and two yearly planners. Ever since the school closed on Thursday and evacuations began, the two had mined through their kids' notes and various textbooks from the bookstore trying to reverse-engineer a continued curriculum.

"If the schools are going to cave to the liberals," Mason had said, "then we'll just homeschool the kids."

Their kids Gray (who was eight) and Louie (who was six) were out in the backyard goofing off around the swing set. Quentin Revere sounded through the countertop radio in the kitchen behind Sara and Mason, railing about the Naomi Perry interview.

". . . gotta make the poor, little black girl look like death, all serious, no smiling, as she sits there and tells us how she escaped this hospital overrun with vampires and how they're all coming for us."

"I still can't believe they think we'd be stupid enough to fall for vampires," Sara said, flipping through a third-grade math book. "If you're gonna start a crisis, make it believable. Make it a nuclear strike or AIDS or something."

On the calendar date of November 1st, Sara wrote, *"Gray—Addition with hundreds places"* with her half-chewed pencil.

"No kidding," Mason said, flipping through a grammar exercise book aimed at first graders. "Might as well have said we're being overrun by Easter bunnies with machine guns."

Sara and Mason both laughed at the idea.

"My contact . . . he's an important man who is very high in the government," Quentin spat, the spittle practically coming through the speakers. "He has confirmed to me that Lil' Miss Perry is nothing more than an actress paid by the government. According to my contact, who was able to talk to me under absolute secrecy, Lil' Miss Perry is currently living in a mansion in Los Angeles, and I have uncovered documents proving that she was paid over seven million dollars to help be the face of this fake crisis operation. Because what did she say again? We all need to go *west*. We all need to *evacuate*. Get as far from these things as possible. Go *west*. That's the game plan, folks. Go west to Hollywood! You know, to Liberal Land! Where the government can take your Bibles from you! Take your rights away! Make you utterly dependent on their services! And that's how they get you, folks."

"Take my Bible over my cold, dead body," Mason muttered.

"Amen," Sara said.

"I just can't believe so many sheep lived around

us," Mason continued. "Running from a great, big nothing. Well, at least we'll raise the boys right. Teach 'em the truth that the government won't."

"It's a crying shame," Sara agreed.

The only sounds were their kids laughing and a low, gentle wind.

October 7

Ronald Grady, seated in his recliner, took a sip of wine. Before the school closed and everyone began evacuating, he'd gotten his students largely through *Beowulf*. Now that he had some time to catch up on grading and planning, he decided to give Milton's *Paradise Lost* a reread. Though he knew the poem inside and out (having taught it to college students for over thirty years), he knew a refresher every now and then could sometimes inspire a new insight worthy of class discussion.

His home was situated less than a mile from Wrightsville Beach. The college closed down Wednesday night and called everyone to evacuate. Ever since then, the town had gotten quieter and quieter until now, when there was nobody left except him and his dog Max. Gone were all the deans and Ronald's colleagues. Gone were the cars and the tourists and the neighbors. All that was left, it seemed, was a haunting wind sent by the ominous ocean itself.

He finished the last page of book six, read the argument for book seven, and decided to take a break. Although he'd been considering having the students do some sort of analysis comparing Milton's writing styles in *Paradise Lost* and its less-remembered sequel *Paradise Regained*, nothing was coming to him.

Maybe a class discussion. Definitely not a written response test, he thought.

Setting the book down on his lap, he sighed. It was nearly ten o'clock, but he didn't feel tired. At sixty-three, he usually called it a night around nine, but the dramatic upheaval of the community had him on edge.

Max eyed him from the couch opposite Ronald's chair. Ronald looked up at his German Shepherd and said, "What do ya, say, Max? Wanna go for a nighttime stroll?"

Max immediately lifted his head and started wagging his tail. Ronald got up and grabbed the dog leash from a keyring next to the front door. After putting his own jacket on, he put the leash on Max who was already jumping up at the door, pawing at it like that would open the door faster.

Ronald opened the door and stepped out into the night air. The evening was warm enough that he decided he didn't need his jacket, though there was a steady wind. The night sky was cloudy, and the streetlights glowed bright yellow.

Every driveway and parking spot was completely empty.

After locking the door behind him, he started walking down the road with Max. He figured a walk to the end of the cul-de-sac and back would be long enough for Max to do his business. As they made their way towards the cul-de-sac, the silence began to unnerve him. Aside from the wind and the sound of their own feet pattering against the asphalt, there was nothing else. No cars. No birds. No people. He thought he could even distantly hear the ocean waves lapping up against the shore.

"Got the neighborhood all to ourselves, Max."

Looking at the houses, he started thinking to himself about what the man on the radio had said. About the government scaring all the Christians out of their homes and abandoning their religious identity.

"I wonder how many of these people left their Bibles behind," he mused out loud. Max paid him no attention, having found the perfect spot in someone's flower garden to leave them a present for when they returned. Feeling a bitterness at how foolish they'd been to believe the government's lies and just give up their homes over something as mythical as vampires, Ronald felt no obligation to clean up after Max.

"Yeah, I think we'll hit the beach tomorrow, Max. Yes, I think a beach walk would do the soul some good."

The two walked to the cul-de-sac and stopped at the house situated at the end of it. Ronald saw what looked like blood smeared all over its otherwise empty driveway. Max began to pace nervously and whine. Ronald chuckled.

"Looks like Hollywood's already been here. Saw no one to hoodwink, so they moved on. Absolutely hilarious."

With another chuckle, Ronald turned and led

Max back towards their house.

October 7

"Why the hell haven't they put the fire out yet?" Leonard said, looking out the bay windows of his living room. He and his wife lived in a two-story home in Morganton with an elevated view of the mountains. It was nighttime, but what had begun as a forest fire the previous night had now grown into a monstrous inferno that illuminated their mountain view with hellish shades of orange and red. It might as well have been a sunrise.

He tapped a finger on his glass of wine, took another sip, and continued staring at the encroaching flames.

This is too close for comfort, he thought.

Kim came into the room dressed in white pajamas and carrying her own small glass of red wine.

"What'd you say?" Kim asked.

Leonard gestured towards the distant fires. "The fire doesn't even . . . it doesn't even look like they've done anything with it. I don't see any airplanes dumping water or anything."

"Well, you heard why," Kim said, standing next to him. "That guy on the radio said the government started the fire."

Leonard sighed. "I just can't believe they're going to burn all this just to stick it to the Christians. Such a waste. Like, who cares? Let them believe what they want. They're not hurting anyone."

"They're really going all in on the vampire hoax," Kim said, taking a sip of her wine. She set her glass down on the coffee table next to the window. On the table, Leonard had already set up the framed portrait his real estate group had given him at his farewell party. The picture had Leonard, Kim, Gerard, Benjamin, Helen, and Michael posed for a group picture on a golf course. The words, "We'll miss ya, Old Timer!" were scribbled on it in black marker.

Leonard shook his head. "Didn't they say it started because of a car crash or something? The fire, I mean."

"That's what the local news said," Kim replied. "But they got that story from the government. The guy on the radio, though. He's right."

"Oh, yes. What's his name . . . Quentin Revere?"

"Yeah, him. He calls it like he sees it. They're just letting the fire burn to take care of any other people who didn't fall for the vampire malarkey. People like us."

"Shit. Guess we're gonna have to leave at some point, then, aren't we?"

Kim shook her head. "This isn't right. They're forcing us out of our home!"

Leonard put his hands on his waist. "I spent twenty-three years building up our lives here, and I'll be damned if I'm going to spend my retirement letting the government burn it all down."

The flames had already reached a frightening height and expanse of the forest. Leonard could see flakes of ash raining down all around their backyard.

Plumes of smoke billowed up over the fiery mountainsides, blocking out any view of the moon.

"How long has the light been on?" Kim said, pointing to their right.

Leonard looked over to where she pointed. Through the sliding glass door windows, he saw that the motion lights had been activated. He didn't see anything in the darkness outside though.

"Odd," he said, moving towards the living room shoe closet. Opening it, he reached high up on the shelf and pulled down his hunting rifle. It wasn't unusual for deer in these parts, but he'd dealt with enough assholes to know that people were capable of anything during a crisis. Things like breaking into fancier homes, for example.

He moved over to the sliding glass door and looked out. He saw the side yard, dark beyond the beams of the motion lights. He squinted, trying to make out anything moving in the darkness.

"I don't see anything," he said.

"Maybe it was a deer?" Kim suggested. "Or a fox?"

"Maybe," Leonard said, still looking. "I wonder if the heat or the ash triggered it somehow."

He moved back to the bay windows and looked out at the fiery mountains again. Kim suddenly grabbed his arm and pointed in the direction of the fires. At first, he didn't see what she was pointing at. He saw the nearly two and a half acres of flat backyard that met with the tree line that began the forest. Then he saw them. Just short of the tree line, someone was running towards their house in a full sprint.

Leonard was a little stumped. There were no major roads in that direction. Maybe a few backwoods trails, but otherwise this person was running from the mountains themselves, running away from the flames.

"Should we help them?" Kim asked.

"Turn out the lights," he whispered. "I don't want to invite some country trash inside. Probably looking to steal something." They turned the lights off to the living room. The motion lights went out on their own a few seconds later. Kim double-checked to make sure the front door was locked, then came back to the bay window.

"Christ, he's not stopping, is he?" Kim asked.

"No, he sure isn't," Leonard said, holding his rifle up. "Stand back a little, hon. If this guy tries to break in, I'm gonna have to do something unpleasant."

As Kim stood back from the window, Leonard squinted out at the darkness. He could now see that the person was dressed oddly for a midnight run in the forest. He had a uniform on with a protective helmet.

"It's a firefighter!" Leonard said. "What the hell is he doing out here? Fire's the other way, hot rod!"

But the firefighter wasn't stopping. If anything, he looked like he was speeding up and intending to charge right through their house.

"He's coming right for us," Kim whispered, moving away from the wall and cowering against the far end. "He's gonna break in!"

"Like to see him try," Leonard said, readying the rifle. He backed up and aimed his gun at the window in case the man tried to break in. The firefighter's head was now in the crosshairs.

The man ran headfirst into the bay window, but Leonard never anticipated what happened next. He never heard the shattering of glass as the man slammed into the window. Instead, the man somehow passed through the window like a ghost and was now crouched on their floor like a cat, hissing and snarling. His firefighter uniform looked singed and blackened in areas as if it had spent some considerable time in flames. The window remained intact.

Kim screamed.

Leonard was too dumbfounded by the man who had seemingly magicked his way into their living room to aim the gun and use it immediately. That split-second delay was all the time the firefighter needed to claim his prey.

Both of them.

The gun was never fired that night, and the mountain fire raged on.

October 8

Neil Bouchillon tossed an oversized denim jacket to Thomas, his seven-year-old son. Thomas, seated on a burgundy-cushioned pew, reluctantly put the coat on.

"I'm not even cold," Thomas complained.

"Stop whining, Tom," Neil said. "Until I get back

and figure out how to turn the heat on, it's gonna get cold in here." He turned his attention to James. James wandered around aimlessly by the altar and observed the giant wooden cross situated above the choir chairs.

At the moment, they were the only three in the church. There were two sections of pews on either side of the sanctuary that created a pathway leading directly from the front doors to the altar. The front pew had a few boxes of clothes and supplies they'd brought with them. Otherwise, they had the whole church to themselves.

"Alright, boys. I'm gonna help your mom with the groceries," Neil said. "This might take a few minutes or a few hours, so let's review. When do we go outside?"

"Never," Thomas grumbled.

"We can't go outside ever," James said, not looking at his dad.

"When do we turn on the lights?" Neil asked, putting on his own jacket and eyeing James.

"No lights. Just use the candles when it gets dark," Thomas said, standing up and walking towards James.

"And use the candles sparingly," James added, sitting down on the altar steps but still not looking up at his dad.

"Use them in a small area away from the windows. Okay, what do we do if people walk in?" Neil asked.

"Tell them we're defending the church from the

government," James said, picking up a rifle from the altar steps. "Ask them if they'll join us."

"James, look at me," Neil said. James finally looked up at his dad. Thomas sensed there was some unspoken communication the two were having just by looking at each other. He often saw his dad have these kinds of looks with his mom in the same way. Whatever it was, Thomas figured this next point was more for James than him.

"James, what do you do if the government walks in?" Neil asked, his eyes narrow and urgency in his voice.

James smiled and held the rifle up. "Tell them to go back the way they came or KABOOM!" He started aiming like he was about to shoot some imaginary intruder.

"Jimmy!" Neil said sternly. "That's not a toy. I'm trusting you to take care of your little brother while I'm gone. Can I trust you? Can I trust you with that? Can I trust that you'll use that responsibly?"

"Yes, sir," James said, putting the rifle back down on the stairs.

"I mean it," Neil said.

"Yes, sir," James repeated.

"Alright, boys. I'll be back soon."

Neil turned to leave, but Thomas stopped him. "Dad, what if something happened to Mom? She's been gone for three hours."

"Your mom's fine. God's keeping her safe. He's watching over all of us because we're being faithful to Him. It's just difficult to find stores open with everyone running away. She just needs some help. I'll go find her, then we'll have some groceries and food for a while."

"How long are we going to stay here?" Thomas pressed. At first, he thought moving into the church would be fun, but now that they'd been here for a whole day, he found the place itself to be rather boring. He missed his own bed, his toys, the sounds of cars driving by outside his window. The stained glass illustrations of Jesus, lambs, and the Crucifixion had long since lost his interest. He just wanted to go home now.

"We'll stay as long as it takes to defend this place. Remember, no going outside," Neil said, finally turning to leave. Their dad walked through the front doors and was gone. Thomas thought he heard the click of the doors locking. Turning around, he saw James standing at the pulpit reading something.

Then Thomas looked at the rifle laying on the steps. Their dad had been very clear that only James was allowed to use it. Thomas sat back down on the front pew and started flipping through a hymnal book to try and keep busy until their dad got back. But he couldn't stop looking back up at that rifle. Now he saw that James was eyeing the rifle as well.

Thomas started wishing that their dad had taken the rifle instead of leaving it.

October 8

Ronald Grady got Max into the car and drove to

Wrightsville Beach to catch the early morning sea breeze. After parking, he slipped the leash on Max and stepped out into the parking lot.

There was something really inspiring about the lack of other people. The only sounds were the ocean waves and the wind sweeping over the dunes. There were no tourists coming in and pissing all over everything, no drunken college students leaving beer cans everywhere. No out-of-town families yelling at their crying children. It could almost be heaven.

Even before they left the parking lot, Max seemed on edge about something. His eyes were fixated on the boardwalk ahead. The sand dunes shielded the ocean from view. Sensing his dog's nervousness, Ronald bent down and pet Max on the head.

"It's alright, boy. Everyone's just gone. We got the whole beach to ourselves today. Who's a good boy?"

Ronald and Max climbed over the sand-strewn boardwalk. The sea breeze greeted them with a welcoming mist that cooled their faces. As they moved past the sand dunes, the dark-blue ocean became visible. Its waves lapped the shore with a moderate roar. It was almost as if the beach were applauding Ronald for staying behind to protect the country's natural Christian heritage.

Rather than enjoy nature's validation, he froze. A chill of terror suddenly gripped his spine, rooted him in place. Max also stopped.

There were at least a hundred or so bodies splayed all over the beach, face down, and surrounded by blood-soaked sand. Several bodies were twitching, but most were not moving.

Max growled, then barked.

At once, about twenty of the bodies lifted their heads in Ronald and Max's direction and shrieked an unnerving sound not unlike what he imagined the demons made when they fell from Heaven. Ronald covered his ears in fright and turned to run, accidentally dropping Max's leash in the process. Before he could leave the boardwalk, he felt something heavy shove him to the ground from behind.

His knees banged the wooden slats. He tried to brace for the fall with his arms, but they ended up getting caught under him as he landed, twisting and breaking on impact. He let out a cry of pain as he felt knees and hands pinning him down. One hand shoved his head down against the cold, wooden boardwalk.

He saw Max bolt back towards the car. Then he felt something sharp and burning pierce his neck.

October 9

"Mase, where are the kids?"

It was Monday around four in the afternoon. They had finished four hours of homeschooling that morning (Mason working with Gray on some cursive writing and Sara working with Louie on his vowels). They sent the kids outside to play after lunch while they graded their kids' worksheets. Mason had gone to watch TV after finishing with the grading.

"They still outside?" he asked, sitting up on the couch.

"I don't see them," Sara said as she looked out the kitchen window.

"Hang on," Mason said, grabbing his shoes. After slipping them on, he ambled over to the kitchen door. Poking his head out, he called, "Gray! Louie! Where you at? Come inside!"

He scanned the backyard from left to right, but there was no sign of the two boys. The old swing set was empty with its swings gently swaying to the light wind. He looked up at the oak tree near the back wooden fence, but they weren't up in that either.

Where the hell are those kids? he thought to himself, stepping out into the backyard. "Gray! Louie!" he called again. There was no response. Now that he didn't hear his kids, he realized how disturbingly quiet it was. He'd gotten used to not hearing anymore cars, but now it dawned on him how there were no animals either: no birds, no dogs, no squirrels scurrying about the leaves and up trees.

Alarmed, he moved to the front yard. *Probably screwin' around down the street somewhere,* he thought. Once in the front yard, however, he looked up and down the street. All the other houses were empty. There were no cars out since everyone had evacuated.

But he saw no sign of Gray or Louie.

"Sara," he called. "I don't see the boys."

Sara came outside through the front door. "You don't see them?"

181

"No."

"Gray! Louie!" Sara began shouting.

"Louie!" Mason called. The only sound they heard was the wind blowing through the autumnal leaves on the street.

"I'm gettin' the truck. We'll drive around and see if we can find them," Mason said, running back towards the front door.

"Should we call the police?" Sara asked, following closely behind him.

"No. I don't want them knowing we're still here," he said. Going through the front door, he snatched the keys from the keyring and went back out. He didn't bother locking the door behind him. "Besides, those doughnut-munching chicken-shits probably skipped town, too," he added.

They both hopped in his black truck that was parked in the driveway. Sara put her seatbelt on, but Mason didn't bother as he turned the keys in the ignition. The truck turned on as the engine rumbled. As he sat back up and shifted the gear stick to back out, he about jumped out of his skin when he glanced out the window.

Gray stood right there looking in at him.

"Jesus Christ!" Mason shouted. Sara was already throwing off her seat belt and hopping out of the truck. Throwing the gear stick back into park, Mason opened his door and climbed out.

"Gray! Where's your brother?" he said but was taken back by what appeared to be a thick coating of blood running down the front of Gray's shirt.

"Oh my God!" Sara said. "Gray, whose blood is that? Are you hurt? Where's your brother?"

Something else wasn't right. Gray's expression looked blank, like he'd just returned from a war he'd rather forget. Gone was the usual, hyperactive child they knew. And his eyes were glowing white.

"Gray, where is Louie?" Mason repeated.

Gray still didn't say anything. Then, faster than Mason could react, Gray opened his mouth and clamped down on his father's neck. Mason screamed as two hot, burning fangs sunk deep into his flesh. He reached up to push his son away, but Gray was surprisingly strong. As Mason pushed on his son's head, Gray only sunk his teeth in deeper.

This is fake! This isn't real! The government got to my sons! were the last lucid thoughts Mason had as Gray finally released him. Mason slunk to the ground, clutching his neck. He heard Sara screaming behind him and was only vaguely aware of Gray lunging at her.

The burning sensation coursed down his neck and into his chest, into his stomach, down his legs. He couldn't make out what was up or down. His mind was going blank. His arms twitched against the cold pavement.

The darkness finally took him as Gray sank his fangs into his mother's neck, pinning her against the hood of the truck. As Mason's eyes went dark, he glimpsed the pumpkin they'd set out for Halloween sitting on the porch. Louie had carved it to look like a smiling face with vampire fangs.

*

October 9

Pancake meowed loudly.

Bertie Zuckerman stopped strumming his acoustic guitar and turned his head in the direction of the kitchen.

"What are you doing, Pancake?"

The cat kept meowing. Setting his guitar down, Bertie got up from his brown recliner in the living room and walked towards the kitchen. He passed his model tramp steamer on the kitchen table and glanced down at it. The base coat of paint was almost dry, at which point he would paint the finer details like rust and decay.

Bertie walked into the kitchen where Pancake sat by the back door.

"What's wrong, buddy?"

Pancake darted his head between the door and Bertie, never stopping the meowing. Bertie looked down at Pancake's food and water bowls. It looked as if Pancake hadn't touched either one.

"Buddy, I've already fed you dinner. You want some lettuce?" Bertie reached in the fridge and tore off a piece of romaine lettuce from a bag. He dangled it in front of Pancake, but Pancake persisted in meowing and kept looking out the door.

"Something out there?" Bertie asked, dropping the lettuce in Pancake's food bowl and moving to the door. Through the window, he saw only an empty alley between his house and the neighbor's side yard. The late afternoon sun was starting to dip down past the neighbor's house. The wind kicked up a little and sent some loose scraps of trash and leaves flying through the alley. Other than that, he didn't see anything worth worrying about.

"Pancake," Bertie said, getting annoyed at the incessant meowing. "You've got your dinner. I scooped your litter box. What do you want?"

Pancake just meowed some more.

Bertie slammed his hand on the counter. "Quit it!"

Pancake stopped meowing. He looked out the window, then back at Bertie, before slinking away to the dining room. The cat hid under the dining table and faced the door, looking no less alert than before.

"Yeah, that's what I thought."

Bertie went back to the living room and picked up his guitar. He hadn't picked it up since before his bar review days.

Maybe I could pick up music again. Maybe.

He made peace with the cat by nightfall. Just before going upstairs to bed, he went over and pet Pancake on the head. Pancake hadn't moved from his spot under the dining room table.

"Night-night, buddy."

Pancake looked at him as Bertie stood back up and headed up the stairs to his bedroom.

Don't go crazy now, amigo. That cat's your only friend. Everyone else jumped town because of the hoax. God, I can't wait to rub it in their faces. Falling for a hoax. Bertie chuckled to himself at the thought of Morris, his boss, coming back looking shamefaced for reacting to a story about vampires.

The cat would sometimes curl up against him in the middle of the night, so Bertie left the door open a crack in case Pancake wanted to come in. Climbing into bed and turning off the bedside light, Bertie closed his eyes. There weren't any sounds outside apart from the brief gusts of wind making shrill wails in the trees. Scattered moonlight filtered through the window. Very soon, he was asleep.

Bertie awoke to find Pancake at the end of his bed looking at him with eyes glowing white in the moonlight. It was still dark outside. Rubbing his eyes, he looked over at his alarm clock. It was 2:14 AM. When his eyes adjusted to the dark more, he looked back at Pancake, whom he now realized was somehow standing over the bed and had the shape of a man cloaked in shadows.

He realized too late that it wasn't Pancake.

October 10

Marsha Waterstone kept turning the radio dial, but all she heard was static. Quentin Revere had been gone all day, and it seemed as if most everyone else on the radio had called it quits too. Gone was the local news. She couldn't find any national news. The commercials, the music, Quentin . . . everything was gone. It was just static radio hissing. No matter how she adjusted the antennae, she couldn't find a signal. All the stations on her television were blurry and out as well.

The last thing Quentin stated was that he and his

family were having to take an emergency trip to LA to tend to his sick father, but he hoped to be back in Nashville soon to keep broadcasting.

"In the meantime," Quentin had said, "we're gonna play reruns of our show for you so more people can hear the truth!"

That had been yesterday morning. There had been no reruns since. Only static.

She couldn't believe it. She stayed because of the reassurances this man had given her that it was all just a hoax to attack Christians like herself. Now he was running, too. She felt her fears of danger come back. Sick father or not, Quentin seemed to think maybe there was something more to the disappearances after all. Even though she herself hadn't seen anything yet, so what? It was a big state. Maybe her house just happened to be the lucky one that was overlooked.

"That bastard just ran," Marsha grumbled, seated at her kitchen table and too overwhelmed to really break down. The pumpkin she'd started carving lay half finished before her on the table. "Lied to us and just ran away like a little bitch." She turned to Delilah, who had come into the kitchen and slumped at her feet.

"Well, D, we've been hoodwinked by a charlatan. Pumpkin might have to wait." Abandoning the radio, Marsha walked towards the back of her kitchen until she reached the pantry. Opening the pantry door, she reached up on top of the highest shelf, groping around until her fingers landed on the cold steel of her revolver.

Pulling it down, she went over to her junk drawer and found a few spare bullets.

"Better to be prepared, D," she said to her dog, who eyed her worriedly. "Whether the dead have risen or it's just a damn trick of the government, we're all alone out here. And that's when the crazies start lootin' and comin' for us stragglers."

She loaded her gun with five bullets in all. The sun was going down and casting an orange-red glow on the walls. As she looked back at the pumpkin sitting with a half-carved smile on the table, she chuckled softly to herself.

Should've carved a vampire face, she thought.

October 10

Thomas looked up from the comic book he'd been reading. He'd found issue #4 of *Alabama Greg and the Dark Blue* in the Youth Group room. James paced around the pews aimlessly, humming a song to himself. The sanctuary air was cold, and even though it was still light outside, the sun was no longer shining through the stained glass windows. The white walls looked bluer than normal.

Thomas shivered a little and pulled his coat tight around him.

"He's coming back," he tried again.

James laughed. "Keep telling yourself that, fat boy."

"I'm not fat!" Thomas shouted.

James shushed him. "Do you wanna get caught?

Someone can still hear us."

"Whatever. He's still coming back. You're just trying to scare me."

"It's been two days, Tom. Something happened to him."

Thomas took a deep breath, wanting to scream but knowing that could attract strangers. "Dad just got hung up. He'll be back. God wouldn't let something happen to people defending his church."

James laughed. Shaking his head, James paced towards the front altar. "Yeah, yeah. God's got the whole world in His hands, doesn't He." It sounded more like a sarcastic joke than a sincere question.

Thomas knew it wasn't like their parents to disappear for a few days like this, but he figured that they'd probably come across some of the bad people and were trying to get back without drawing any attention.

They wouldn't leave us, he thought.

James stopped near the end of the pew Thomas was sitting on. He looked over at Thomas. "You ever wonder if maybe this isn't a government takeover? Maybe it really is vampires?"

"Jim! Stop it!"

James shrugged his shoulders. "Because it seems kinda stupid that everyone would just run away over nothing."

"Dad wouldn't lie to us. He trusted us to defend the church."

"Why?" James said. "Why do we have to defend the church? Why can't he do it? Where is he? He wants to defend it so bad, why isn't he doing it?"

Thomas struggled for an answer. "Because it's the right thing to do. God wants us to."

"How do we know that?" James asked.

"Shut-up."

James laughed. "Okay, don't answer, pudgy."

"Stop calling me fat!" Thomas wanted to hit James now, but James stood there, looking at him mockingly.

"Stop oinking so much, piggy-boy. You're gonna draw attention."

"I don't care! Stop calling me piggy!"

Thomas's yell was the loudest noise either of them had made in a few days. When it echoed throughout the sanctuary, they both instinctively held their breaths and waited for someone to burst in through the front doors and arrest them. But when nothing happened, Thomas went back to reading his comic. He was more interested in Alabama Greg fighting a gang of robots anyway.

James laughed. Looking at the same doors their dad had left out two days earlier, he finally said, "I'm going outside."

"No!" Thomas hissed. "You'll get killed!"

"Better than freezing to death in here. Besides, Dad would want us to make sure everything's good on the outside, wouldn't he?"

Thomas didn't have an answer.

Maybe. But he said don't leave. He said we have to defend God's house.

"Jim, you're scaring me. Don't leave."

James laughed. "Aww. Is the scared little piggy

190

too afraid to be alone for a little bit?"

Thomas got up to hit him, but James shoved him to the ground. "I'm older, so I get to leave. Got it? You stay here."

"Shut-up! We can't leave!"

James reached down and slapped him across the face. Then he stormed over to the altar, grabbed the rifle and marched back to Thomas. "I'm going outside. I'll just be a few minutes, maybe a few hours. You can stay here and cry like a baby. I don't care. I'm looking for Mom and Dad."

Thomas started to cry. "Don't leave me!"

James laughed. "Good God, you really are a crying, little baby. Little Tommy cries like a piggy? Oink-oink?" Laughing, he began pointing the rifle at Thomas. "Little Baby really want something to cry about?" He put his hand near the trigger.

Thomas screamed. "Stop it! Stop it! Oh my God!"

"I could pull this trigger and kill you," James said, almost to himself. Thomas curled up and screamed for him to stop aiming the rifle at him.

James shouted, "Boo!" and jumped like he was going to pull the trigger. Thomas flinched and screamed even louder, crawling away frantically and cowering against a pew. James laughed. Lowering the gun, he said, "Look at you. Crying and crawling around like a little baby. God is laughing at you right now. You're no mighty warrior for God."

Thomas didn't say anything but kept crying.

James slung the rifle over his shoulder. "I'm going

out. I'll be back." James then marched to the front doors, leaving Thomas crying under a pew. He unlocked the doors and passed through them. The doors shut behind him, and soon the only sound was Thomas crying.

October 10

Marsha Waterstone sat on her front porch with her dog and revolver, listening for any sounds. It was dark and quiet now. Aside from the occasional rustle of leaves by the wind and the gentle creaking of her rocking chair, there were no sounds anymore. No cars, no people, not even crickets or birds. The whole neighborhood had gone dark. Her house was the only one with the lights still on.

"World's gone to Hell in a handbasket," Marsha said to Delilah, who slumbered at her feet. Delilah grunted as if in agreement. Marsha just continued to stare out into the darkness of the night, daring any backwoods hick or idiotic juvenile to come mess with her.

Marsha wasn't aware of the two vampires that had snuck into her house through the back. She didn't see the three on top of her roof as she went back inside to get ready for bed.

Entering through the door, she froze when she saw the two vampires standing in her kitchen, their eyes glowing a hideous white and their teeth dripping with blood. They glared at her with rage and hunger.

"You're intruding in my home, Satan. Begone!"

192

Marsha said, aiming her gun at them. Without hesitation, she sent the one on the right's head to Kingdom Come. His body fell to the floor. The one on the left paused, then crouched down like a cat ready to pounce.

"You don't impress me," Marsha said, aiming the gun at him. He let out a snarl, then leaped at her with blinding speed. He knocked over a chair as he lunged. Marsha pulled the trigger and watched as his shoulder exploded. The arm fell limp as the rest of him fell, snarling. Delilah was now barking and running back into the kitchen.

The vampire got back up though.

This time she shot him in the head. As his body fell limp, she turned to lock her door behind her.

"Goddamn it," she said, staring at no less than twelve vampires standing on her porch, eyeing her hungrily. The nearest one casually walked through the door like a phantom unencumbered by the laws of physics. He moved towards her, savoring each step towards his delicious meal as she backed up into the kitchen. Looking at her, he smiled, baring two large fangs. The ones behind him looked even more ravenous with blood dripping from his teeth.

She looked at her revolver, opened it, counted the bullets she had left, then closed the chamber.

Two bullets.

"You ain't gettin' no pleasure from me," she said. Aiming the revolver at her skull, she pulled the trigger.

*

When James returned to the church, he hadn't found their parents. When Thomas asked what he saw out there, James simply muttered, "Not Mom or Dad," and sulked off. In the day since James had returned, he hadn't said much else to Thomas, and something resembling peace settled over the sanctuary.

It was early afternoon now. As Thomas sat on a pew rereading his comic book, James suddenly flew into a rage at the altar. He stormed onto the stage and overturned some of the choir chairs, yelling and screaming.

"What?! What?!" Thomas said, alarmed and getting up. If Thomas pointed the gun at him again, he would run outside. He didn't care if his dad got mad.

"Useless! Everything!" James stormed into the backroom, then came back with a bucket of paint and a paintbrush. Dropping them near the wall behind the choir seating, he stormed over to the cross and kicked it down. Splintering at the base, it clattered on the ground with a deafening clap.

"Jim! Be quiet! Someone'll hear!"

James laughed. "No, they won't. You know why, piggy? Because we're the last ones here. The last, stupid ones here."

"You're scaring me again," Thomas said, feeling his tears rise up once more.

"Oh, you're scared? What about me?!" James

shouted. "You think I'm doing any better? You think I don't know what's happened to Mom and Dad? You think I don't know how we're going to die here? Tom. We're dead. We are going to die, and it's Mom and Dad's fault."

"No, we're not! We have lots of food left," Thomas said, but James scoffed and marched back up to the altar.

"Talking about the blood, man. Bloodstains everywhere, Tom. Up and down the streets. And we're next.

Through tears, Thomas screamed, "Stop it!" but James just laughed and made his way over to the back wall with the paint can. As he popped the paint lid off and dipped the brush in, he began singing "Amazing Grace" in a mocking tone, really emphasizing his disdain for the words *sweet, saved, wretch, lost,* and *see.*

With the brush, he began painting letters on the rear wall in big, red strokes. Thomas sat down on the pew and wanted to argue, but he knew James knew more than he did. James had gone outside. James knew what was out there. And whatever it was, James had snapped and said they were going to die.

James continued a frenzied, screaming rendition of "Amazing Grace," each verse getting more hysterical and deranged as his mocking increased. Thomas pleaded with him to stop shouting, himself shouting the pleas, but James ignored him and continued painting on the wall. Thomas looked at the front doors, scared that something would burst through them at any moment.

Then he heard James scream at the top of his lungs. Turning around, he saw James fling the paintbrush out towards the sanctuary and stomp towards the rifle leaning against the pulpit. Grabbing the rifle in one hand, he went into a sort of military marching stance. On the wall behind him were the words *GOD IS NOT HERE* painted in bright, red letters.

James made a mock-salute with his free hand and began marching in place. "Look at me, Dad! I'm a soldier for God! Aren't ya proud of me? Aren't ya, Dad?" With that, James pointed the rifle at the ceiling and fired four shots into it, screaming like an action-movie hero as he fired them. Thomas screamed and ducked under a pew, horrified at how loud the gun was and at how terrifying his brother had become.

Flecks of the ceiling fell to the carpet. Even though he was out of bullets, James kept clicking the trigger and screaming until he finally gave up and threw the rifle to the ground. He sat down on the stairs leading up to the altar and slumped over, looking at the now useless rifle. He chuckled softly to himself and said, "Dad didn't even leave us extra bullets."

Thomas crawled out from under the pew and stood up.

"Jim," he said, but then he heard a noise behind him.

It was over near the front doors.

Turning around, he didn't see anything other than the front door wide open. The early afternoon air wafted in, cooling Thomas as it reached him. He eyed the door, hoping it was just a strong gust of wind that pushed them open.

"Jim, are Mom and Dad dead?" he finally asked, still looking at the door.

James nodded, but Thomas didn't see this. The doors slowly swung until they closed. Thomas turned and watched his brother, who looked like he'd just given up and was waiting for sweet chariots to take him home. James had his face in his hands, staring blankly at the floor.

"Are they dead?" Thomas asked again.

James nodded again.

"What's outside? What did you see?" Thomas asked, feeling a sinking feeling in the pit of his stomach.

"Death," James replied simply.

Thomas turned back towards the front door. Something sounded like a low, hissing sound, but he didn't see anything or anyone. He started backing away from the pews and sat on the steps near James.

"You know, I've been thinking," James said. "Might be kinda cool to be a vampire."

"What?" Thomas said, horrified.

"Think about it," James said. "Live forever. Can't be killed as easily as a normal person. Turn into a bat and fly around."

"What about drinking blood?"

James shrugged. "Guess you wouldn't have to worry about what food you were going to eat, would you?"

"Doesn't the sun kill vampires?"

"I think they can walk around in the sunlight."

"But vampires aren't real!" Thomas said. "Dad said the government made them up!"

James looked at Thomas. "Tom, there's like five of them in here already." He pointed up, and Thomas looked. Sure enough, there were what looked like five men crawling on the ceiling like cockroaches, looking down on the two boys with malevolent, white-glowing eyes.

"They're waiting for us to run. The moment we run, they'll pounce. I saw one of them do it when I was out," James said.

"Will God protect us?" Thomas suddenly screamed, feeling foolish even before blurting the question out. He knew they were both about to die.

James laughed, looked back at his painting on the wall, looked back at Thomas, and shrugged. "You can pray if it'll make you feel better. Maybe God will have mercy on us as vampires."

Thomas began to cry.

"I'm sorry I have no better words," James said, a tear starting to form in his eye.

Blinded by fear, Thomas bolted towards the front doors. A deafening shriek from above filled the sanctuary, and suddenly something very heavy landed on his back. He fell to the ground, screaming as he felt the vampire bite into his neck. He heard James screaming somewhere behind him.

As Thomas felt his blood being sucked out of him, he glimpsed a radio on the floor near the doorway. It was their dad's radio.

Dad's favorite radio. The one he listened to all the time. His favorite was that show with the man who said there were no vampires.

Thomas was then dragged back underneath a pew where he heard more vampires snarling.

GIFTS OF THE HARVESTER

On the cool and breezy afternoon of the 18th, Paige stood looking out at the ocean. Waves clapped down on the cold sands, and gray clouds stretched across the blue sky. It looked almost like a watercolor.

She wasn't quite sure how she'd gotten there. She remembered being at a hospital. She was waiting for something. Someone. The doctor. The x-rays. Then there were the screams. She remembered the screams and the explosion. She remembered the scary man bursting into the room and lunging at her.

What followed was a blur of nothingness mixed with nightmares of wandering a wasteland, feeling a burning hunger and thirst within her after waking up. It drove her to seek out new blood. She'd scavenged every day. She knew she'd slept, though she couldn't remember when. She knew that she slept better on the nights when she'd tasted blood than when she didn't. When she didn't, she had the nightmares.

But now she stood at the ocean.

She recognized it.

Virginia Beach.

She used to bring her daughters here during the summer.

My daughters, she thought. *I wonder where they are.*

It was the first time she remembered having a lucid thought in over two weeks that wasn't fixated solely on finding blood to drink. The faces of her daughters slowly came back to her. She tried to remember their names.

Ashley.

Brittany.

I can't remember the oldest one. She had blonde hair, like me.

Images of running and carnage came to her now. She remembered the patient in the next room. She remembered the nurse in the hallway. She remembered the victims along her long trek to this beach. She'd been ever driven by a relentless thirst, but something else had driven her to this place as well.

She remembered the screams of her victims, but there was no guilt. Just . . . confusion. *What happened to me?* she thought. *Why am I here? Why can't I remember my daughter's name?*

She remembered this place always made her feel at peace. Perhaps that's what drove her here. She hadn't known peace since that awful night in the hospital. The only peace now came from the blood.

I had a husband and three daughters. What was his name?

A word came to her, something from childhood, that seemed to describe what she was.

Vampire.

It seemed like such an inadequate word now, something invented to frighten children. It couldn't capture what she now felt. She felt that she could order this ocean to part if she so chose. She walked towards the crashing waves.

Stepping on a broken glass bottle brought her out of her thoughts. Looking down, she saw a clear shard of glass had punctured straight through her pale, bare foot. Blood seeped out. It didn't really hurt. It stung, but she felt more annoyance at the incident than pain. Reaching down, she shoved the glass out of her foot. Setting her foot back down on the cool sand, she stared at the wound for a moment.

She sensed that something wonderful was going to happen.

She wasn't disappointed. After a few minutes, the puncture tear seemed to congeal itself, then rapidly scar. Within ten minutes of standing there, there was nothing left of the wound except for some dried blood and a faded, white scar.

I am powerful.

She looked up at the ocean. Beyond the crashing waves, it looked dark-green and somehow calm.

Can I cross this?

She stuck her hand out. The waves continued crashing onto the sand, heedless of the woman experimenting with her newfound powers. The water splashed her arm. In a different life, she'd have thought the water was freezing. Now, she didn't mind the cold as much.

I wonder, she thought.

She walked into the ocean, trekking past the breaking waves and into the deeper waters. Seashells crunched under her feet, but they didn't hurt her. Though the waves pushed her and splashed her torn and ragged hospital gown, she did not feel as if she had exerted any energy. A riptide pulled on her, and she let it carry her out. When she was able to roll free, she found that she could swim as naturally as ever.

I guess I haven't lost all of my humanity, she thought. *I wonder, though.*

She let herself sink into the depths of the sea. The water closed in above her head, drowning out the sounds of wind and rushing water. Now she heard only the steady deep hum of the ocean waves rumbling overhead. She descended perhaps eight feet before landing on the underwater sands. She opened her eyes and saw the murky green depths around her. Lots of seaweed and floating shell fragments. Here and there fish swam about, darting away if they got too close to her.

She smiled.

She didn't have to hold her breath. In fact, she didn't have to breathe at all.

Her lungs felt as if they had been replaced by something more assured and reliable. She laughed underwater, amazed by this new power. Water entered her, but it did not suffocate her. With a deep inhale, she vomited the water back out with no sensation of drowning.

She no longer lived on air. She lived on blood.

It's not a curse. It's a gift.

She rose to the surface and began swimming east. After several hours of this, she felt as if she had exerted no energy at all. She felt she could keep going until the end of time. Coming back up to the surface, she turned around to see how far she'd swum. She couldn't see land behind her anymore. Turning back around, she wondered how far she could get before she started to feel the call of blood.

The call to fight off the nightmares.

In the distance, she spotted a boat. From this distance, it looked like a small yacht. It was hard to gauge exactly how many miles out the boat was from her. Someone had probably gone out for a joy ride, or maybe they were trying to escape the chaos by living out on the ocean.

Perfect. Dinner and transportation.

She began swimming towards the boat. She already had designs to feast on its crew and use the boat to cross the Atlantic. With her newfound ability to exist underwater in ways no mere human ever could, finding fish for sustenance would not be a problem.

She intended to see Europe. Perhaps she could enjoy the harvest there first before anyone else.

THE BURNING PAINTING

I stand at a high overlook of the valley. Down below is a city and the surrounding mountains, all in flames. I have been here most of the day admiring the work of my children.

When I first heard of the fire starting, I made my trek up to the mountains to get a better view. I am glad that I did. The mountains no longer radiate green and blue but instead glow red and yellow, scorched beyond salvation. The towns and neighborhoods burn as well. Ash rains down. Aside from the distant crackling of the inferno, there is a palpable silence only disturbed every now and then by some unfortunate soul who has just been discovered by one of my children.

Occasionally, I hear an explosion in the distance, probably from a fire reaching a gas line or a tankard. No one puts the fires out since there are not many people left anymore. Plumes of smoke reach the heavens like violent brush strokes from an artist obsessed with the colors red, black, and yellow.

It is a glorious inferno that would have made Her proud. I see something poetic in it. The old world burns away, and our world begins. The autumn rains will be here soon, I am sure, to deal with this fiery purge, though I cannot help but smile as I watch the city below burn away with the landscape.

This is beautiful.

I remember the paintings in my old home. Once upon a time, my father had many. Of all the skills I have taken up over the past century, painting was not one of them. Just the thought of those paintings awakens a yearning in me to return to those ancient halls. This great burning below could easily have been the main attraction of that collection.

I cannot, of course, ever return. That life is far behind me. That schloss and those paintings are no more, existing only as memories.

"I wish you were here, Darling," I say out loud to the blazing breeze, knowing there will be no reply.

I do wish She could have seen this painting. I know it would have delighted Her, especially since I am what She once was. I would point out the intricate screams and violent textures to Her as our children continue to grow the kingdom, forever perfecting this painting. This one would have gone well in our collection.

Instead, I must content myself to watch the portrait unfold alone, watch it burn as they once burned my Beloved.

In quiet moments like this, whispers of the Great Nightmare crawl back into my soul, torturing me with the future and whispering those questions about who I am. I can never know the answers to them, of course. Not without Her.

One question burns brighter than the others

today. I have often wondered why other people turn so quickly when it took me several years. I was dead and in the ground for some time before I reawakened, yet my children turn within hours, sometimes minutes.

After all this time, I can still feel the needle-like punctures She left in my breast, which have long since scarred over. It is the only physical reminder I have of Her.

I have long been aware of how the venom works. It took practice, but eventually I learned to either withhold it or offer it as I pleased. The more venom I inject, the faster it courses through my prey's body. A steady jet of it can turn one within hours, yet a single drop can take months to fully take hold.

So why did Her venom take years?

It is a riddle that has baffled me endlessly. In that brief season we had together, She visited my bedchambers. She stole Her fill of my blood when I slept, but She never drank to the point of my death. In our final days together, I began showing signs of turning. She must have injected me with some by then, but it had to have been a very little bit, practically microscopic, to finally take hold years later after I had died.

Why?

Why did She inject me with the venom after so many nights where She was content merely to taste my blood?

I clutch my chest and sit on the edge of the cliff as I recall those painful days. So many conflicting images and sensations mar that season. There were the terrible things: Her rare tempers, the visage of a demon coming to me at night, my sickness, the truth of Her identity, and Her horrible scream when they killed Her. But there were also Her sweet affections and embraces, Her moonrise confession, the flutters in my own heart that I dared not utter then, our evening in the secret passageway, and what we did there.

In the years after they killed Her, when my condition worsened, I withheld these more intimate moments from the doctor. In those days, such things were kept hidden, so I opted to reveal only the confusion She made me feel. It was far easier to play up their fears of a vampire's seduction than to openly wrestle with feelings that he could never understand. In hindsight, those feelings of confusion were akin to one who has discovered something wonderful but does not yet know what it is.

Like the first person to discover fire. What must they have thought?

What is fire?

Is it magic?

Is it safe?

Is it dangerous?

Can I touch it?

It was only after I returned from death that I knew I wanted to touch that fire again, but I could not. They had killed Her, and She was gone forever.

Like those paintings, She was nothing more than a memory. The few conflicting recollections I have of Her now scream at me one conundrum almost as loudly as the Great Nightmare screams.

Did She love me, or did She only want my blood?

The sun is setting. I rise. Night will fall soon, so I must resume the hunt for more sustenance. I will not be greedy. As my children are born, there become more mouths to feed. I can take only what I need to stave off the Great Nightmare while they learn to control their new agency. Most people have left by now, but there are a few idiots left who think we do not exist. That was a miracle I could never have foreseen. There will be more feasting as we make our way West.

Something behind me approaches.

Small feet shuffling along the asphalt.

Spinning around, I see a little girl standing in the empty road. Her curly blonde hair is disheveled and dirty. Her purple shirt depicting a horse is matted in thick, dried blood. She is about eight years old. I smile as familiarity sweeps over me.

She is the girl from the Knoxton house.

Laura.

"What did you do to me?!" the girl screams, her voice a violent tornado of rage and fear and grief. She charges at me, now clawing and punching, scratching and cursing. It does not hurt me, so I take the abuse like one patiently awaiting their child to tire from throwing a tantrum.

She stops and looks up defiantly at me, rage burning out of her pale, white eyes. No matter. Bending down, I look right back. Even as one of my children, the girl is not yet wholly resistant to this spell. She'd have to have an exceptionally strong will to resist it at this stage.

"I have perfected you," I say.

She looks as if she wants to cry but cannot. Anger mixed with hatred blocks any tears. I bend down further and move the little girl's hair out of her face.

"You are growing fast," I tell her. "You have experienced the Great Hunger, but now you are satisfied enough to question why."

"Why?! Why'd you do this to me?! What am I supposed to do now?!" the girl screams.

Calmly, I reply, "You are now my daughter. And you have helped make me more sons and daughters. You are to continue making more brothers and sisters for yourself. That is what you are to do. However, you do not yet realize how powerful you truly are. You will learn in time."

"I don't want this!" the girl screams.

I cannot help but smile.

I remember saying the exact same thing once.

"Not now," I say. "But you will learn to accept it. For now, learn to control your venom. I am sure you have already discovered how to do this."

"I think so," the girl says, her will still defiant.

"Use it to make siblings. Withhold it to feast. The more of us, the harder it will be for them to exterminate us. Once we have vanquished this world of them, their cancerous existence will be nothing but a distant nightmare."

The old pains return for only a moment. I almost feel bad lying to this child. I know this sanguinary path means that we will one day run out of drink, and then we will all suffer a truly eternal torment.

But I am tired of suffering alone. Tired of not knowing the answers.

Did She love me or not?

"Who are you?" Laura asks. She, too, wants answers. Fortunately, I have some for her.

Names are just a tool for others to use as they wish. I have not used my name in so long that it means nothing to me. She was not around to call my name anymore, nor were there any companions, so my name has become little more than another memory.

"I am Mother," I say. Putting a hand on the child's shoulder, I add, "Go forth and make more of us. You are coming out of your infancy as a ravenous beast and into your own as I once did. I suspect others will very soon, too. Remember, Laura, that you are perfected now. Any wound they throw your way will heal. Unless they sever your head, so try to protect your own neck."

This last tip I offer with a wry smile.

The girl looks positively terrified now, but I remove my hand and stand back up, regal and calm as a mother should be. I stare into Laura's eyes for a long while, and finally the girl cowers away and walks back into the darkness of the forest.

Turning back around, I watch the burning painting for a little while more. It looks even more beautiful in the failing sunlight.

"I wish you could see this, Darling. Our children have made such a marvelous work of art. And it is only going to get better."

An idea comes to me, the only shred of hope I have ever known.

Perhaps She preyed on my blood once, but as we became closer, She longed for me by Her side just as I now long for Her. Perhaps that is why She gave me the venom.

But perhaps, too, She also knew the Great Nightmare was as much a burden as a gift. Perhaps She gave me so little venom to prolong my life as much as possible before succumbing to the darkness as a final act of love. Knowing that they would soon find Her and attempt to kill Her, She gave me the venom so that we could someday be together.

It is a pleasant thought.

Without Her here, I can never know for sure.

I turn to leave and rejoin the darkness, never knowing the answers but finding solace in Her actions.

I just wish She was here to enjoy this painting with me.

MERE MORTALS IN A STRANGE HOUSE

Escape was the only thing on Cate's mind as they ran through the forest.

The only sounds were their heavy breathing, the grass and sticks being trampled underfoot, and a low wind. In all directions were trees with the afternoon sun filtering through their mostly leafless branches. The man's screaming ceased, and an unsettling quiet took over. Cate had gotten used to the absence of birds and other animals, so their absence now didn't really faze her.

It felt as if she'd been running for hours, but soon the trees began to thin out, and Cate saw what looked like a neighborhood ahead of them.

"There," the other woman panted, pointing up ahead. There was a small house with blue vinyl siding and a wooden back porch. To Cate's surprise, the back door was wide open and practically begging them to take refuge within.

Emerging from the trees, they crossed a giant backyard. The October leaves lay scattered about the yard.

They both ran up the back porch.

"Go, go, go, go, go! Get in! Get in!" the woman

shouted behind her.

"Shut the door! Shut the door!" Cate screamed, launching herself through the back door and into the kitchen. Hearing the woman slam the door shut and lock it behind her, she finally allowed herself to catch her breath resting against the kitchen sink.

Holy shit. Holy shit. Oh shit. Oh shit. Shit.

Turning around, she saw the woman sitting down with her back to the door, also catching her breath. Cate said quickly, "Did it follow us?"

The other woman turned to look out the door window. Cate joined her cautiously, peering out of the window but taking care to stay hidden from view. They both scanned the yard and the trees. There was nothing. Nobody.

"I think we lost it," the woman said, sounding relieved.

Cate went back to the kitchen sink to catch her breath. The woman remained on the floor catching hers. As Cate leaned on the sink, she noticed the dirty dishes piled up in it. Some fluffy, white mold grew on a bowl of beans, and a thick liquid congealed on a nearby pan. These dishes had been abandoned for some time.

Turning to the other woman, Cate finally said, "Was that one of them?"

"Yeah, that's them," the other woman said. "Your first one?"

Cate nodded, still shaking.

"Yeah, well, there you go. The dead have risen indeed," the woman muttered, standing up. She let her hands rest on her hips and surveyed the kitchen.

"They're a lot faster than I thought," Cate said.

"Too fucking fast," the other woman said.

Cate looked around the kitchen. A pair of wooden crutches caked in a fairly large spatter of dried blood lay on the linoleum floor. The refrigerator sat silently against the wall to her right, which made her wonder if the house had any power. Knowing how awful a fridge without electricity could smell, she resisted the impulse to open it and check. Opposite her was a counter with the stove and a cutaway in the wall revealing the dining room. Next to this was a little walkway connecting the two rooms.

Aside from their breathing, the house was completely quiet. No sounds of skittering mice, no hint of the house's settling foundations. More unsettling was the quiet from outside. No birds, no people, no cars, not even crickets. Just a steady, autumn wind moaning ominously.

Cate looked nervously towards the dining room, afraid something might be hiding around the corner.

"You think anyone still lives here?" Cate said, suddenly cautious about their volume. She didn't want to alert any vampire that might be hiding.

"I doubt it," the woman said, pointing at the bloodied crutches. The crutches unnerved Cate. Coupled with the moldy dishes, it was clear the homeowner had been attacked. Whether by vampires or other people was unclear. But where were they? Had they left? And if so, were they gone for good? Would they return? Or were they hiding in another part of the house, waiting to pounce on unsuspecting strangers like Cate and this woman?

The opened backdoor, which seemed so inviting when they were being chased, now felt like a trap.

The other woman must have had the same misgivings. Without another word, she stepped over the crutches and walked through the dining room, looking around cautiously. Cate decided she wanted to make sure the coast was clear herself.

She saved my life, but I don't know her. What if this is all a trap she set?

Cate cautiously followed the other woman through the dining room. They passed through an entryway on the right that led into a destroyed living room. Despite the bloody mess in the kitchen, it looked as if the main attack had occurred here. Two comfy chairs and a bookcase had been knocked over. Books and picture frames lay scattered all over the brown-carpeted floor. A coffee table was on its side, and the porcelain lamp that once adorned it now lay in shattered pieces on the floor.

Opposite to the entryway was the front door, closed and locked. To the left of it was a wall with a tall, brown bookcase that somehow escaped the struggle. Its books were straight and organized. Three side-by-side windows with their blinds down lined the wall to the door's right. A long, green couch sat unscathed in front of these windows. Over at the far right of the living room was a single window overlooking the driveway. A desk with some papers and drawing utensils sat before it.

They turned left down a small hallway leading to

the rest of the house. There was an old floor furnace in the center of this hallway. Next to it was a small bookcase lined with old books and a sizable collection of picture albums. A large, framed picture of a woman riding a horse hung on the wall above the bookcase.

Before them were three doors. The door immediately before them was open, revealing a darkened bathroom. Cate inched forward into it. Though it was small and hard for anyone to hide in exactly, the shower curtain was drawn.

I hope to God there's nobody behind the shower curtain, she thought.

"Be careful," the other woman whispered. Cate walked into the dark bathroom and resisted flipping the light switch on. If someone was hiding and waiting to spring out at them when they least expected it, they were probably hiding behind the shower curtain. Hating the suspense, Cate felt she had to check.

Worst-case scenario, we're back to running, she thought.

Reaching out slowly, she grabbed the blue shower curtain. With a quick yank, she pulled the curtain open.

There was nobody there. Cate sighed in relief.

I hate this.

Looking in the room to the right of the hallway, they found a guest bedroom: a queen-sized bed made up nicely, a small dresser with a plastic flower vase and the Bible on it, and an empty, open closet. No vampires. No people.

The left door led into the master bedroom. Two closets on the left with bifold doors were both wide open. A pair of pants hung from a clothes hanger on the furthest closet door. There were a few crates on the bed filled with clothes and some toiletries like toothpaste and deodorant.

"No one," Cate said, finally sighing in relief.

"Yeah, no vampires," the other woman said, eyeing the crates. "Look at all this stuff! Think they were planning to clear out?"

"Maybe," Cate said, looking back out the door. She started to wonder if in the time they had spent searching the house, the vampire from the gas station had caught up to them.

What if it's outside now?

"We might be able to use some of this," the woman said, hovering over the crates.

"Knock yourself out," Cate replied, who wanted more than anything to keep moving. As the woman studied the crates, Cate went back to the kitchen. She looked out the backdoor, but nothing seemed to be out there.

"Found some things that might come in handy," the other woman called out a few minutes later. Cate leaned against the sink as the woman returned to the kitchen carrying one of the small crates. Setting it down on the stove, the woman said, "Man, you almost bit it. No pun intended, of course."

"Uh . . . what?" Cate asked, wondering what was in the crate.

"Back at the gas station? Lucky I was there to pull your ass back into the alley. What were you doing, anyway?"

Looking for Sarah, Cate thought.

"I was . . . looking for someone. Well, really just getting supplies and moving west."

The woman brushed her curly, dark hair aside and looked in the crate. "This should help with supplies. We can shore up here for a while, get some necessities, and set out again. Oh, by the way, I'm Bridget." The woman extended her hand. Cate shook it.

"Cate."

Cate had an uneasy feeling about this house. It felt as if it were being watched. The chase was still painfully fresh in her memory, and her instincts to keep running were high. She thought about the man who almost hit them with his car when they were running. The man in the red *Revere Zone* shirt who unwisely stepped out of his car to offer them a lift, heedless of the dangerous vampire chasing them. If he hadn't pulled up at that exact moment, the vampire definitely would have caught at least one of them instead.

Can we outrun those things?

Cate moved forward, careful to step over the bloody crutches, to peer into the crate as the woman rummaged through it. It looked like an assortment of tools and junk with no particular organization. She saw boxes of batteries, rolls of tape, some twine, a flashlight, some small candles, a few rags, and additional items that might once have belonged to a junk drawer.

"Listen, uh, Bridget," Cate said, trying not to sound ungrateful for being rescued. "Thanks for saving me back there, but I think it's best if I keep moving."

"I think the owners were going to evacuate," Bridget said, looking through the crate. "Let's see. We got a flashlight . . . matches . . . got any batteries?" It didn't seem as though Bridget had heard Cate say that she was leaving.

"I mean, I don't think it's a good idea to stay put here. I've been trying to cover as much distance as I can, and there's still a few hours of sunlight left, so I think I'm gonna head on."

Bridget snorted. "You're lucky you've made it this far, judging on how reckless you've been. Okay, batteries and twine. These could be useful."

Cate felt her cheeks flush with irritation. "Excuse me?"

"You almost walked right into a vampire without realizing it. And now you want to keep walking? This whole region is crawling with vampires. Come on, stick around. I'm trying to get out, too. We'll stock up, find some weapons. Two heads are better than one, ya know? Increase our odds of survival." Bridget continued rummaging through the crate.

Cate felt an urge to cuss this woman out.

Doesn't she realize we're still in danger here?

"We can't stay here. It's too dangerous! What if that vampire's still out there?" Cate said.

"Tape . . . wipes . . . a wrap."

"What if it gets inside?" Cate looked out the backdoor window, then back at Bridget. She was laser-focused on the contents of the crate again and ignoring everything Cate said. The fear of being chased again made Cate's heart start to race, and Bridget not listening only angered her.

"Bandages . . . Okay, we got a first aid kit. That's good."

"We aren't safe here!" Cate pleaded. "This place is a deathtrap. Are you listening to me? We can't stay here. We—I—need to get out of here."

"Hello! A cross!"

Bridget pulled out a simple wooden cross. It looked like something one might hang up in a kitschy flower shop. She handed the wooden cross to Cate. "Go outside and hang this up on the door, will ya?" Bridget said.

Cate looked at it doubtfully, not appreciating the sudden order to go outside. "What the actual *fuck* am I supposed to do with this?" she asked.

Bridget rolled her eyes, glared at Cate, and said, "It's a cross. Hang it up on the door. Maybe it'll ward off vampires? Come on, it's better than nothing."

Cate scoffed with a sarcastic chuckle. "Okay, whatever. Daylight doesn't kill them. But sure. This'll do the trick." A part of her, however, really did wonder if a cross offered any protection. Until a few weeks ago, she'd believed vampires were merely the products of European folklore. Now, she wouldn't be surprised if crosses actually had some sort of mystical, vampire-repelling power.

Annoyed, Cate walked over to the door. Bridget pulled a roll of duct tape out from the crate.

"You might want this, too."

Cate snatched the roll of tape and began tearing

off little gray strips of it. Folding them into loops, she covered one whole side of the cross with tape before finally deeming the thing ready to hang up. Moving to the doorknob, she stopped. Cate looked out the window, not trusting for a moment that they were actually safe here.

She knew that silence didn't necessarily mean vampires weren't there. They could be hiding amongst the trees at the end of the backyard, staring at the house and waiting for some sign of life to reveal itself. Not seeing anything, Cate unlocked the door and slowly walked outside.

I've gotta keep moving. But Bridget's right. I need supplies. Need a plan.

Nothing came bursting out of the trees as she stepped out onto the porch. The wooden planks squeaked a little under her step. Otherwise, the only sound that could be heard was a low wind in the trees and leaves.

So far, so good, she thought.

Closing the screen door slowly, she quickly placed the cross on the glass window. Pressing it into place to ensure the tape stuck, she heard a twig snap from somewhere in the woods across the backyard. Whipping her head around, she froze and looked.

It's back!

She scanned the yard. She looked at every tree and at the neighbors' yards on either side. There was nothing. No birds or squirrels. No lurkers watching from the trees. None that she could see, anyway. Just that god-awful silence that reminded her the entire world had turned upside down. The only movements were dead orange and brown leaves blowing lightly across the backyard, never to be raked again.

Slipping back inside the kitchen, she closed the door and hoped the cross would stay put. She didn't have much hope in it doing anything, but as Bridget had said, it was better than nothing.

Bridget carried the crate of supplies into the dining room. Scattered papers, bills, pencils, and cups cluttered the dinner table. A bookcase and an artist's desk lined the walls. Paintbrushes and an open tackle box with watercolors and a stained palette lay out on the desk. Next to the tackle box was an unfinished painting of what could have been a bird or a legume. It could be a giant dick with eyeballs for all she cared. Given their situation, none of these items looked particularly useful to Bridget.

A weapon. Something for self-defense, she thought, looking around the room.

Setting the crate down on the table, Bridget noticed an old-fashioned phone niche in the wall. There was a photo of an elderly couple standing in front of an emerald-green backdrop. Next to it was an older, sepia-toned photo of the couple looking much younger at a beach. A white cord ran down the wall from the niche between the two photos.

As Cate walked into the dining room, Bridget spotted the telephone on the table. She moved past an overturned chair towards it, grabbed the phone, and lifted the handset to her ear. Cate watched eagerly as she listened. After a moment, Bridget slammed it back down on the receiver.

"Damn it," she said.

"Does it work?" Cate asked, leaning against the kitchen doorway.

"Dead tone," Bridget said, looking at her. "Same as everywhere else."

"No phone?"

"No phone. And no calling for help, either."

Cate flicked the dining room light switch up. The overhead light shined on.

"The house has power, at least," Cate said, turning the light back off and taking in the dining room. Bridget noticed a little black box on the floor near Cate's feet. Looking closer, she saw it was a radio plugged into the wall.

"Hey! What about that?" she said, pointing.

Cate looked down and picked it up. The radio was black with some silver bordering around the station dial. The antenna was already partially sticking out. Cate looked skeptically at the thing.

"Is anyone still broadcasting?" Cate asked. "I thought everything went dark."

"I don't know. Maybe?" Bridget said. "Maybe someone out there's still broadcasting. Maybe they've got a plan. We could at least try to get some news."

Cate, still looking unconvinced, shrugged her shoulders and nodded in agreement. "Okay. Better than nothing."

Setting the radio on the table, Cate pulled the antenna out all the way and turned the radio on. Immediately the speakers hissed and crackled, but it was otherwise silent. Cate fiddled with the knobs, turning it to one station, then another, and still another. She cycled through all the possible stations, then reset the knob to the start and slowly turned it, listening for anything resembling a human voice. They heard nothing but static.

"Come on, there's gotta be someone," Cate said. "Anyone." One station had a long, droning whine that didn't stop. As she continued twisting the knob and watching the orange needle scan frequencies, Bridget moved into the living room behind her. Looking out the window, she was surprised to see the sky growing dim. The sun was already halfway down behind the neighbor's house.

She saw a silver car parked in the driveway.

Alrighty then, Bridget thought.

"Cate, come here a sec!" she said.

With a defeated sigh, Cate joined Bridget by the window. "Can't find anything. I left it on, though. Just in case. Who knows? Maybe something'll happen."

Bridget pointed, and Cate looked towards the car. Her face lit up, a little bit of hope replacing some of the fear.

"What do you think?" Bridget asked. "We take the car and get outta here?"

"Sounds good to me," Cate said, eyeing the car intently.

"Alright, we'll need to find the keys first."

"Let's spread out," Cate said, turning around and beginning the search. "They've gotta be around somewhere.

Bridget looked at the car, a worrying idea hitting her. "What if they're in the car?"

Cate cocked her head skeptically. "What kind of bonehead leaves their keys in a car?"

Bridget shrugged. "I've seen some old people do it. I'll go check the car. You look around in here."

"Okay."

Bridget ventured outside through the back door, cautiously looking around for vampires. She didn't see any. She went over to the car and tried opening the doors, but they were all locked. She peered in through the driver's window. She didn't see any keys.

Gotta be in the house, then.

Walking back to the house, she kept her eyes on the forest. Even though there were no sounds or visible signs of vampires, she couldn't shake the feeling that they were being watched. The nervous feeling made her walk faster to the house, more determined to find the keys now.

Please, God, don't tell me they had them in their pocket when they got attacked.

Bridget stopped suddenly. She looked across the neighbor's yards to her left and right, then back at the forest.

That feeling.

She saw no one. She heard only the wind. There was just her, the car, and nothing else.

Had she imagined it?

Images of the young man on the bridge came back to her. The older man at the gas station. The screams during the hellish nights of hiding and wandering.

The woman in black in the parking lot.

She felt exposed.

We need weapons, Bridget thought.

Cate scanned the living room for the keys. The mess wasn't the only thing complicating the search. The carpet was an unsightly brown shag, which meant the keys could be buried somewhere in the fabrics. That was assuming the keys were in this room at all.

Bridget walked back into the living room and leaned against the dining room doorway. Cate continued searching, but after a few moments she noticed Bridget still standing in the doorway. She hadn't moved to help search at all.

"Are you gonna look for the keys?" Cate asked.

Then she realized Bridget was deep in thought, concern clouding her whole face. Her arms were folded, and her breathing had quickened.

"Cate, I think we need to find weapons."

Cate glanced out the window towards the car. It would be getting dark soon.

The longer we stay here, the greater the danger, she thought.

"What's wrong? Did you see one?" Cate asked.

Bridget shook her head.

"Whether or not we find those keys, we're still defenseless," Bridget said. "Without any weapons, we're as good as dead anyway. Look, I don't know. Maybe we find the keys, maybe we get outta here.

Maybe we end up lucky and escape those things. But not if . . . not if we run into *her*."

Cate paled. A cloud of palpable despair suddenly fell on the room.

"Her?" Cate asked.

"If she finds us, and we have nothing to fight with, we're as good as dead," Bridget said.

"Who are we talking about? Who's *her*?" Cate asked.

"I don't know, but she's one of them," Bridget said. "I saw her. She wears all black. Like a black cloak and a black robe. Like some sort of homeless cult member or something. I don't know who she is, but she's important somehow. You'll know she's near because she gives off a feeling."

"What kind of feeling?" Cate asked, her tone growing quieter.

"A bad feeling. It's hard to explain. It's like this sensation that your doom is right around the corner, and you've already lost the opportunity to save yourself." Bridget wrapped her arms tighter around herself.

"You think we can kill them?" Cate asked, her voice betraying her growing dread.

"I think they can be hurt," Bridget said. "I saw one on a bridge a while back. His legs looked torn pretty badly. I thought he was just an injured teenager needing help, but he was a vampire. He was pretty fast, too. He chased me."

"How'd you kill him?" Cate asked.

"I didn't. He saw a deer and attacked it instead, so

I was able to get away. Barely. The point is he had injuries."

Neither one said anything for a moment. The static of the radio was the only sound keeping them in the present. Finally, Cate said, "So, weapons and keys?"

"Yeah," Bridget said. "Yeah, I think so."

"Okay," Cate said.

Cate continued searching in the living room while Bridget turned to the dining room. Looking around, it was clear the most threatening objects here were paintbrushes. Beyond jamming them in a vampire's eyes, Bridget didn't think these would be that useful.

She moved to the kitchen and began opening drawers, looking for cutlery.

Spatulas . . . dish towels . . . junk drawer . . .

Finally, she pulled open a drawer to the right of the sink. Here she found the silverware, some measuring spoons, and an assortment of knives. She grabbed the most formidable one she could find: a sharp, wooden chef's knife about the size of her forearm.

This'll do for now, she thought. Turning, she resumed searching for the car keys.

Cate saw nothing in the living room worth calling a weapon, so she turned down the hallway and headed into the master bedroom. Looking in the closets, she couldn't find any box or compartment that might conceal a firearm. There were some old shirts and numerous empty wire hangers, but no

229

weapons. No guns, no hunting rifles, nothing.

Were these people pacifists?

She was about to give up, but upon turning around she noticed a wooden baseball bat wedged in-between the crates on the bed.

Good enough for me, she thought and grabbed it.

Having a weapon didn't exactly make her feel much better. The chase earlier had left her shaken, but a different feeling started growing once she put up the cross on the back door. It started small, but it hadn't gone away. In fact, it had only gotten worse, especially since Bridget had mentioned the woman in black. She didn't want to tell Bridget, but it felt sort of like an impending doom around the corner, and the opportunity to save herself was already gone.

The radio suddenly cracked to life.

"There's no one left," a woman's voice said, startling them both. They ran to the dining room. Cate adjusted the antenna a little to reduce some of the hiss. Bridget listened intently with a chef's knife at her side.

"That's good, you got it," Bridget said. "Don't lose it!"

Cate let go of the antenna.

The woman on the radio took a deep breath and sighed. "Everyone is either hiding or cleared out before things got too bad," she continued. Chuckling to herself a little, it sounded like she was taking a puff of a cigarette.

"The studio is overrun, listeners, so now I'm

speaking from my goddamn basement. Yeah, I said 'goddamn.' Who the fuck's gonna stop me now? Producer's a vampire. Janitor's a vampire. Censors are all vampires. Well, let's be honest. I mean, the censors were always vampires. And then my co-host got his throat ripped out and now he's a fucking vampire and just . . . shit."

There was a long pause. Cate felt that foreboding sensation growing. She noticed Bridget holding herself again, looking at the floor. Whatever nerve they'd had earlier was fading.

Can she feel it, too? Cate wondered. *Is that woman she mentioned nearby somewhere?*

She glanced out the dining room window at the failing late afternoon light but didn't see anything other than trees swaying in the wind.

"I'm sorry," the woman continued, now sounding overwhelmed to the point of crying. "I think this is the end. In case anyone's listening, this is—"

Here the woman assumed a performative tone.

"—Mama MacDaddy! Reporting Live from her basement!"

Static hissing.

Then she spoke again.

"Consider this my farewell broadcast. My fucking swan song. Sixteen years on the air. It's been a good run. Never thought it'd end like this. Anyway, what happened? Our studio got overrun. I was getting ready to do another morning show with my co-host, Randall. Y'all might know him as Randy Daddy-O. But his real name was Randall Sheridan. We studied communications together in college. We were also part of an improv troupe. It was in that improv troupe where we came up with the personalities Mama MacDaddy and Randy Daddy-O. For those of you living under a rock, my real name is Josie MacAdams. When we graduated, our act got the attention of old Josh Faun. Remember *The Josh Faun Show*? Same morning slot. He liked our act so much that he invited us on the show. It was such a hit that he asked us back on, and the act became a staple segment. When Josh Faun retired, we got offered the show, and the rest is history. *The MacDaddy and Daddy-O Show* was born, and later we became *Mama MacDaddy's Mixtape*."

Cate looked at Bridget. Bridget shrugged. "Never heard of them."

Cate nodded. "My roommate listened to them sometimes on the morning commutes. Morning radio shock jocks. Kinda juvenile. I think more for teens, maybe? I didn't really listen to them."

"So why am I giving you the history lesson?" Josie continued. "Because I wanted to honor my friend. My co-host, Randall Sheridan, was attacked by a vampire one morning. We were set to start just like any other normal day. We were covering the hospital thing. God, that feels forever ago now. Yeah, yeah, we should've evacuated when we had the chance, but they asked us to keep things light while the national news covered the vampire outbreak, so we kept playing music. Anyway, vampires broke into the studio and killed just about everyone. I barely got out. I couldn't get to the car. There were so many of them. Hundreds. Just running around, jumping anyone they could find. I don't know how the fuck I got out. But Randy didn't make it."

Josie sighed, the despair in her exhale clear.

"Honestly, from where I'm standing, this is it. This is the end."

That feeling of dread intensified within Cate. There had been some hope that maybe there was a plan. Something. Anything. Surely this radio host with connections knew something. Surely she could convey some news.

"I haven't seen or heard from another human being in two weeks," Josie continued. "I'm here in my home studio broadcasting. Don't think anyone's gonna mind if I take over the airwaves now. We set this up in case I had to do a show from home. Never thought I'd have to do it because of fucking vampires. So . . . yeah. Here we are. Everything's gone dark. Last I heard, the president went missing, and I guess it's safe to assume there is no functioning government anymore. Everywhere is just . . . dark. All you can do is survive now. Survive until you play the losing card. It's gonna happen eventually, so might as well sign off soon."

Bridget wrapped her arms tighter around herself. Cate clutched a nearby chair for support. This was not the message they were hoping for. There was no plan. There was no one in charge. There was just defeat, plain and simple.

"I can feel that sensation," Bridget said, terror creeping into her voice more and more with each passing moment. "That feeling that she's near."

Cate nodded slowly. "Me, too."

"Consider this my farewell broadcast, listeners," Josie continued. "I can hear them coming now. They're upstairs. They're not trying to be coy about it. They want me to know they're here. They want to fuck with my head some. Well fuck 'em! You can't see this, but I'm flicking them off with both hands. For myself, for Randy, for all mankind!"

Another pause.

"I wish I could give more comforting words. I wish I could say they die out by daylight or are driven off by wolfsbane or some folklore shit like that, but I can't. Because they're not. It's funny, in a way. We have all these silly vampire legends and stories, and we always gave ourselves easy ways to kill them off. Man, do we look really stupid now. Like those scientists from the 1900s who thought exposure to more radium was actually good for you. One generation's wisdom is another generation's cautionary tale."

A sound like a banging door followed by otherworldly screaming made Josie begin to shout faster.

"If you can get out, get out! Get out! Fight them! Don't become a victim of this plague! Don't let them win!"

The sounds of vampires hissing and snarling drowned out her words. The speakers popped as if something kept hitting the microphone. They heard what sounded like clothes or maybe flesh tearing violently. The snarling and shouting continued without interruptions.

"Get out! Save yourself! Get the fuck off me!"

The woman screamed frantically, but then she suddenly stopped. All that could be heard was the sound of snarling and hissing.

Bridget turned the radio off finally.

Cate looked up at her.

"We need to get out of here," she said.

"We need to find the keys," Bridget said.

The sun was no longer visible, and they still hadn't found the keys.

They searched through every drawer, cabinet, closet, dresser shelf, crate, counter space, even trash cans, but the keys still eluded them. Cate turned up the chairs and overthrown furniture in the living room, hoping that perhaps the keys had somehow gotten lost underneath them, but they weren't here either.

Finally, it was too dark to continue looking. They both agreed that turning on the lights would only draw attention if something was out there, so they retreated to the kitchen in near total darkness. There was no moonlight to help them see, but thankfully their eyes had mostly adjusted to the dim house.

They found some peanut-butter and bread in one of the cabinets. When they discovered that the fridge worked after all, they found a jar of muscadine jelly. After pouring some water from the faucet into glasses, they drank and ate some sandwiches quietly in the darkened dining room.

That oppressive feeling hung over them like a suffocating blanket. Not knowing if there were vampires lurking outside added to the sense of dread. But there was nothing more they could do. They were going to have to spend the night in a strange house together and wait until morning to resume the search, or maybe even continue on foot if they couldn't find the keys.

"Who is she? The woman you mentioned earlier?" Cate finally asked in a hushed voice.

Bridget lowered her sandwich and didn't say anything for a few moments, chewing in silence. Cate sensed that Bridget was recalling something even more unpleasant than the gloomy feeling they were both experiencing now. Finally, Bridget said, "I saw her in a grocery store parking lot. Probably over a week ago."

"What grocery store? Where was this? Were you evacuating?"

Sitting up and looking at Cate more fully, Bridget spoke in a quiet whisper. "I was a fire lookout. Didn't know things had gotten real bad until after the fire started. I mean, they had reported all the people going missing on the radio, but I spent my watches usually reading books. I didn't listen to the radio much. Didn't talk to anyone really. I liked it that way. I was reporting on the fires that had started, and I guess I didn't realize how bad things had gotten until my contact stopped responding to his radio. By the time I decided to get the hell out of there, some asshole had stolen my car. I was pretty much stranded, so I had to take one of the park's four-wheelers and go as far west as that could take me. When that ran out of gas, I started walking. Been walking ever since. Found empty houses to stay in each night, restocked food as best I could, and set out again the next day. Gotta say, not having a car really sucks the big one."

Cate didn't say anything. As she listened to Bridget, she thought about her own travels after losing the car.

It's not really lost. It's upside-down and totaled in a ditch somewhere outside Woodbury, she thought glumly. *Thanks, Mr. Semi-Truck.*

"I saw a vampire one day," Bridget continued. "That guy on the bridge. The one I tried to help? God he was so fast. He would have caught me if it hadn't been for a deer standing there. He got distracted by the deer and went after it instead of me. Just like that man today. If he hadn't been there, that vampire might've gotten us."

Cate didn't say anything. She wanted to forget the chase.

"I'd never felt that close to death before," Bridget said. She took another bite of her sandwich and chewed it, thinking. Swallowing, she continued. "I knew I'd have to be careful going forward. So I moved slower, hid more, surveyed the roads before continuing on. I imagine you've had to do the same?"

Cate nodded. "Yeah, pretty much. I haven't seen anything until today, but yeah. Hiding in homes. Getting food."

"Yeah. You know the drill. Thing is, you're the first normal person I've come across in over two weeks. I haven't seen another normal person since before the fire. It's been hell, to say the least. I always enjoyed my solitude, but I can actually say it's really good to find another human being." She took another bite of her sandwich. As Bridget chewed, Cate worked on her own sandwich, and her mind drifted to Sarah.

"Honestly, though, the worst parts have been going to sleep," Bridget continued. "Breaking into strange homes, hoping to God there's not some lunatic with a gun waiting to blow my head off, not knowing if I'll wake up with a vampire hovering over me the next morning. I mean, nowhere's exactly safe anymore, is it? But you know what I mean. I find some random bed to sleep in and try to get some rest when all of the sudden I hear screaming. Dead of night, no sounds, then suddenly someone down the road is screaming. Every now and then I'll hear one of those creepy-ass vampire screams they make, too. That's why I stopped sleeping in beds and started sleeping in closets, or under the bed just to hide better. It's nerve-wracking."

Cate thought about the howl the man at the gas station made when he chased them. The memory of that sound and the terrifying chase afterward reminded her how lucky they both were to be alive.

Bridget sighed. "One day, as I was moving west, I felt the presence. At first, I didn't realize what it was. I just had this feeling, this intense dread that at any moment, something would leap out and kill me. Like what we're feeling now."

"Yeah," Cate agreed.

"At night, I've had horrible nightmares about getting killed by vampires. Nightmares that seem so real in the moment. But waking up, the dread is still there, so there's barely any relief to realize it was just a dream. During the day, that feeling never really leaves. Sometimes it softens, or I just get numb to it, but most of the time I feel scared. Like unbearably terrified to even move. I just have to mentally force myself to keep moving, to keep chasing those moments when the dread weakens a little."

Bridget took the last bite of her sandwich. Cate didn't say anything. If this feeling was anything to go by, she thought she understood why Bridget was having difficulty talking about the woman in black.

"So, one day I felt the presence. But this time, it was much stronger. I felt like I couldn't move. I was paralyzed with fear. I was walking past a grocery store. I looked over and standing there in the parking lot was this woman all dressed in black. Black cloak. Black robe. Long dark hair down to her waist. She was standing over a dead body."

Bridget wrapped her arms around herself again.

"I don't know who she is. I just felt this feeling . . . it comes from her. Don't ask me how I know. I just knew then and there that it was coming from her. I felt like I was about to die. Even though I was hiding behind a bush, I felt like hiding wasn't enough. I could just . . . feel . . . this immense, heavy hatred coming from this woman. I think the only reason I was able to leave at all was because she left first. She walked away."

Shaking her head as if trying to forget an awful memory, Bridget said, "I pushed myself to keep moving. I got the hell out of there as fast as I could. I mean, I don't know who she is, but she made me feel like a little insect in her world, a little insect that's only alive because she allows it. I knew I had to get away. And I had to be careful. Cautious."

Cate didn't say anything. She finished her own sandwich and tried to forget the feeling of dread that had settled over the room. She wondered if the woman was near. Unless they went outside to check, there was no way to know for sure.

"Anyway, that's my story. How'd you end up here?" Bridget asked.

"I was at a family reunion in Kentucky when the shit hit the fan. But I had to drive back to get my college roommate. She—we—had an argument right before I left."

"What'd you argue about?" Bridget asked.

Cate didn't feel like dredging up how it had started over a simple debate of whether they could afford a shared computer. Sarah wanted to use the world wide web, but Cate didn't think it was in the budget. The disagreement led to other things that had been simmering, such as Sarah always bringing over guys who helped themselves to Cate's food. Cate leaving the lights on when she wasn't using them. Sarah listening to loud music whenever Cate tried to study for an exam. Cate not doing the dishes quickly enough.

It culminated in Cate storming out and calling Sarah that word.

Cate decided to give Bridget the short version.

"It was over something stupid like whose turn it was to do the dishes. Anyway, I wanted to make sure she got out okay. We argued, but we've been friends since middle school. I didn't want to leave our friendship with a stupid argument when the whole world was falling apart. I had to make sure she was okay. When I got back, the whole town was evacuated. There was nobody left on campus. She didn't have a car. No note or anything. Her backpack wasn't there, but I couldn't tell if she had packed up and left with someone else or not. I hope she got out. I decided to stay the night."

"Wait, you went to a family reunion when everything was going down?" Bridget asked.

"No. I was literally getting in the car to come back when all hell broke loose," Cate replied.

"Where was this?"

"McMinnville."

"Okay."

"So, I took off the next morning," Cate continued. "Figured I'd head west and hopefully find her. Evacuate in the meantime."

Apologize for everything I said.

"I got somewhere near Woodbury when a semi-truck came out of nowhere and sideswiped me. Knocked the car upside-down."

"Damn," Bridget said.

"Yeah. I mean, I was fine, but the car was trashed. The driver just left me for dead. Didn't stop. I

241

climbed out with some scrapes and bruises. I had to keep moving west, so I just kept heading on and spent each night at a new house. Abandoned houses, I mean. Been doing that for a few days now. Not sure how long it's been."

Bridget looked down at her half-finished sandwich. "You don't know if your friend got out?"

Cate shook her head. After a moment, she added, "You know, if I'm being honest with myself, I think I stopped really trying to search for her after the third night. Because if she did get out, she's probably already out west, safe and sound. And if she didn't get out . . . well, there's nothing to be done about it."

And I'll just have to live with that word being the last thing I ever said to her.

Bridget looked up at Cate. She didn't say anything, but Cate sensed something in her eyes that suggested understanding more than what had been said. Bridget ate the rest of her sandwich in silence. Cate sat there and didn't add anything, hating herself, hating the way she'd treated Sarah, hating how completely and utterly the world had collapsed seemingly overnight.

Bridget finished her sandwich before saying, "For what it's worth, I'm glad I ran into you. It was getting to be too much doing this alone."

Cate nodded. "Yeah. Me too."

They found a bulb of garlic on the cutaway wall between the kitchen and the dining room. Crushing it up, they sprinkled it on the floor near the backdoor. The aroma reminded Cate of eating spaghetti at a nice restaurant. She doubted it would do anything, but it somehow made her feel a little better.

They decided to stay together in the living room. They could hear any intruder attempting the front door more easily. If someone tried coming through the kitchen door, they could escape through the front door. As Bridget peeked through the blinds of the living room window, Cate returned to the master bedroom.

She'd rummaged through enough of the stuff in this house to know where the spare blankets and pillows were kept. Going to the closet with the pants hanging from its bifold door, she pulled a box from up on the shelf. Setting it on the bed, she pulled out a blue-and-white falsa blanket and two small pillows. Underneath these was a larger and fluffier blue blanket.

She carried the blankets and pillows back to the living room, where Bridget stood looking out of the window blinds. The sky was dark, and there were no streetlights to illuminate anything, so Cate asked, "See anything?"

"No," Bridget said. "It's too dark to say for sure, but I don't think anything's out there."

"Here," Cate said, setting the dark-blue blanket and pillow down on a chair. She retreated to the corner near the front door with her falsa blanket and pillow in hand. She'd already leaned the wooden baseball bat against this corner. Setting up a makeshift bed, she laid down and tried to get comfortable, clutching the bat for protection. Bridget began to spread out her blanket and pillow closer to the window. As she did so, she asked quietly, "You scared?"

"Yeah." Cate pulled the blanket over her. She was exhausted both mentally and physically, and she just wanted the night to end.

"Me too," Bridget replied, fluffing her own pillow and settling in with the chef's knife by her side. Cate decided not to say anything further, clutching her baseball bat and trying to find a comfortable resting position. Lying parallel to the wall, her feet just barely touched the bookcase there.

"I guess there's one upside to being afraid," Bridget added.

"What's that?"

"It heightens our sense of survival. Makes us more alert. Well, more alert than if we didn't think there was any danger." Bridget said no more, and soon there were absolutely no sounds beyond the moaning wind outside.

Cate pondered Bridget's words.

It's like a game of survival. Like a fucked up game of cards. Each decision either gets you killed or lets you live a few minutes longer. Two to four players, all ages.

As the quiet took over, her mind wandered to Sarah. She tried not to imagine Sarah as a vampire now roaming the streets looking for blood.

I hope you know I'm sorry for what I said, Cate thought. *Wherever you are, Sarah, I want you to know how sorry I am. God, I never should have called you that word. I don't know what I was thinking.*

Nestling against her pillow, Cate's eyes wandered

around the dark shadows of the living room. Bridget's eyes were closed, and she seemed to have already drifted off. Cate was exhausted, but that tight pit in her stomach that warned of danger lurking outside just wouldn't go away.

As something approaching drowsiness began to set in, she noticed a spiderweb in the corner of the ceiling directly above her head. A black spider hung motionless on it, perhaps also not wanting to draw attention to itself.

Maybe I can convince it to write nice things about us on its web and convince the vampires to spare our lives, she thought glumly. She shut her eyes and tried to sleep.

Outside, darkness blanketed the neighborhood. The clouds obscured what little light the waning crescent moon had to offer, and the streetlights were all out. There was no sound beyond the wind pushing leaves down the street.

No cats meowing, no stray dogs howling, no crickets chirping.

A wolf spider sat motionless on the cross Cate had taped to the back door. No other creature could be seen. The wind ceased, and silence fell over the neighborhood.

Without warning, the wolf spider scurried up the door and hid itself behind the head jamb. It raised its fangs to defend itself.

Dread seized Cate out of her nightmares. She sat up and looked around the room, her heart beating quickly in her chest. Nothing looked noticeably different. It was still dark. Bridget slept and breathed gently, which was the only sound to be heard. But that sensation of dread was suffocating now. This was no longer an unpleasant feeling. Every one of her instincts screamed at her to run, that danger was upon them.

Goddamn it, she thought, looking up. The spider was nowhere to be seen. She looked at Bridget, who looked fast asleep.

Cate didn't know what the danger was. More importantly, she didn't know *where* it was. It seemed to be getting *closer*, however, and the oppressive sensation grew with each passing moment. Cate tried to steady her breathing, fearing that if she breathed too loudly, it would attract whatever was causing this feeling.

Is it the woman in black?

Suddenly the baseball bat felt as useless as a butterfly net. The dreadful feeling that something—or someone—was lurking right outside made her heart begin to race. She remembered the vampire at the gas station and how quickly he ran after them. That had been during the day. What chance would they have of escaping in the dark? She started thinking of the exits: the front door or the kitchen door. Both would require fast moving, and both led out into the unknown night.

It would all depend on where an intruder entered.

What if it's already inside? What if it came in while I was asleep? What if there's more than one?

A few minutes passed, but nothing happened.

There was no sound. But that dreadful sensation grew.

Bridget hadn't stirred.

Cate heard herself lightly whispering, "Bridget! Bridget!" But it was more of a barely audible gasp than an outright whisper. She didn't dare speak too loudly.

Where is it?

Cate thought of all the places she could hide if escape proved impossible. The master bedroom. The guest bedroom. Under the beds. Behind the shower curtain.

This house is a deathtrap, she realized. No place was safe here.

Suddenly, a glass window in the kitchen shattered with a loud smash, crashing onto the floor. The noise jolted Cate into action. Bridget also awoke and sat upright, clutching her chef's knife and looking like she'd woken up to somehow find herself in a lion's den.

Grabbing her bat, Cate crawled over to the doorway where the living room met the dining room. Peeking around the corner, she could see into the kitchen. Her eyes adjusted to the darkness enough to detect a large pile of glass shards scattered about the floor. The glass came from the now broken backdoor window. The cross she'd hung up earlier now lay in two pieces in the middle of the broken glass heap.

A light mist began seeping in from the direction of the back door. Cate felt death surround her. She almost turned for the front door, but a sudden thought flashed into her mind.

There could be more outside!

Without another thought, she dashed blindly towards the master bedroom. She climbed into the furthest closet and closed its bifold doors behind her. As she tried to quiet her breathing, all she could think about was the feeling of dread. It throbbed inside her skull now, like an infernal drum signaling doom.

It came for her now.

She held her bat close.

Bridget was out of options before she even knew what was happening. She'd been having nightmares of the woman in black, so the sensation of fear saturated her sleep without her realizing the danger was actually real.

The glass shattering woke her up, but it wasn't until she saw Cate scrambling to the back rooms that her head cleared up enough to realize, *I'm fucked.*

The woman was here.

Bridget immediately felt transported back to that parking lot where the woman feasted on some innocent man. She felt that same paralyzing fear that made moving difficult.

Gotta hide. Gotta hide!

She darted behind the couch and squished herself as closely to the wall as possible. It wasn't a good hiding spot, but she hoped to God it was good enough.

Peeking out around the edge of the couch arm, Bridget looked at the dining room doorway. At first, everything looked dark. Nothing seemed to be moving in the darkness, and there were no sounds. Then, just when Bridget began to hope that maybe there was no intruder after all, the woman in black swooped in from the dining room, silent as a distant cloud.

Just as before, she was cloaked all in black. Her dark hood was up, making her look like a phantom burglar. Her face was pale in the darkness, and her fangs were bared for feasting. Her eyes seemed to move between pitch black and glowing white. The woman stopped at the doorway and raised her head, as if trying to sense something rather than seeing it.

She's hunting us! Bridget thought fearfully. *She knows we're in here!*

The woman looked at the blanket and pillow left on the floor where Cate had slept. Then she scanned the living room. Bridget shrank back against the wall, willing her heart to stop pounding so loudly. She didn't dare take a breath. Any sound could give her away.

Bridget sensed the woman looking at her blanket and pillow now. The oppressive feeling felt stronger as if actively trying to choke her, make her gasp for air. But she held her breath.

Suddenly, the noise of clothing falling to the floor travelled from the direction of the bedrooms.

The aura of dread lessened. Bridget sensed the woman turning her attention towards the back of the house. Risking a peek, Bridget looked around the couch and saw the woman move swiftly down the hallway towards the master bedroom.

Cate!

*

Cate forgot about the pair of jeans hanging from the closet door. At first, she didn't realize what happened. Once she heard it, all she registered was a noise. But then the wave of despair washed over her all anew, and she realized that the dreadful presence was coming towards her.

Then she remembered the pants hanging up. She'd hastily closed the bifold doors, not realizing that this would dislodge the hanger. She kicked herself for missing them, but it was too late now.

The sound got the intruder's attention.

They were coming her way.

Cate held her breath and clutched the bat.

I'm so sorry, Sarah.

Bridget felt the malice alleviate slightly as it was no longer directed towards her general area. As she watched the woman disappear into the shadows of the hallway, her eyes landed on the bookcase against the wall where Cate had slept.

Something on the bottom shelf caught her eyes, barely discernible in this dark room but catching just enough light to reflect a faint, bronze glint. Although it was very dark, Bridget saw clearly enough to realize what she was looking at.

The keys!

They were barely visible and all but blended in against the books behind them, but there was no doubt: those were the keys they'd been searching for. Since the bookcase seemed untouched by whatever violence took place before they'd arrived, they hadn't paid too much attention to it. The keys were sitting in the right corner of the bottom shelf, easily overlooked by even the most desperate searchers. From her position, it looked like a small ring with a few keys.

For a brief moment, she forgot her danger. There was a glimmer of hope now.

Get the keys. Get the hell outta here.

Cate heard very soft footsteps approaching. They were almost imperceptible if not for the overbearing silence.

The fear was so palpable now that tears started running down her cheeks. She didn't make a sound, but deep down she knew it didn't matter. This thing knew she was in here. The dreadful sensation made her want to fling open the closet doors and beg for a quick death just to get it over with. The idea of turning into a vampire even started to sound appealing.

Maybe it'll turn me into a vampire. Maybe then I can kill it with vampire abilities.

A dark shape walked in front of the closet door where Cate lay hidden. What little darkness Cate's eyes had adjusted to was now blotted out by this creature standing on the other side of the door.

Cate heard a soft chuckle.

A woman.

She *knew* Cate was in the closet.

Cate clutched her bat as the shape moved to pull open the bifold doors.

Bridget crawled quickly and quietly towards the keys.

They were almost in her grasp.

Bridget knew she could grab the keys, sneak out the door, start the car, and be gone from this place. Anywhere was better than here in this oppressive gloom.

What about Cate?

She was in reach. She grabbed the keys, clutching them tightly to prevent them from jingling. Then she pressed herself flat against the right of the bookcase, hiding from view of the hallway. In her other hand was the chef's knife.

Gotta save Cate. Cate's gonna die!

Bridget grabbed Cate's pillow and flung it into the dining room. The pillow landed against a chair, causing it to scrape across the floor and break the silence.

She immediately felt the vampire's aura coming back towards her now.

The woman started to open the closet door but stopped. The woman suddenly moved back out of the room towards the living room. Cate felt the oppressive sensation shift away from her. A noise had drawn the woman's attention.

Cate dared a quick breath of relief.

Bridget!

There was no time to unlock the door and bolt through it to the car outside. Bridget could only hide and hope the vampire would follow the noise into the kitchen rather than look around the bookcase.

She heard soft footsteps fall on the other side of

the bookcase and pause.

Although she couldn't peek around the corner, she knew the woman in black had returned to the living room. The intense dread suffocated her. Bridget was trapped. Much like the couch, this was a terrible hiding place. If she ran, she was dead. If the woman simply looked around this bookcase, the vampire would kill her.

Bridget clutched her knife, ready to plunge it into the vampire's chest as a last resort. She didn't know if that would kill the woman or not. But she had no other options.

Suddenly the aura of dread shifted again.

Bridget sensed the woman walking away.

She's . . . she's leaving?

Risking a peek around the corner of the bookcase, she saw she was right: the woman in black moved back through the dining room and into the direction of the kitchen.

She's following the sound! She fell for it! Now's my chance! Cate, get the hell outta there!

With the woman moving to the wrong part of the house, Bridget saw a painfully narrow window of escape.

Out the door. Start the car. Get outta Dodge.

Cate even had a slim chance to escape now, though Bridget didn't know how to warn her without alerting the vampire also.

Maybe Cate'll hear the car and get out, too.

It was risky, but it was now or never.

She waited a few seconds until she was sure the woman was in the kitchen. Standing up slowly,

Bridget held up her knife and braced herself in case the woman came running out of the darkness back into the living room. She heard nothing, and the dining room remained dark.

I'm outta here.

Bridget turned to unlock the front door.

There stood the woman blocking her exit, as if she had magically teleported there.

"What the fuck!" Bridget shrieked, but it was too late. The woman grabbed Bridget's head with terrifying strength and screamed that unearthly howl. This close to the vampire, Bridget smelled her foul breath, hot and sticky. She saw her serpent-like fangs, sharp and long.

Quicker than lightning, the woman jammed her teeth into Bridget's neck. Bridget's nerves ripped and burned. She felt her vocal cords cry out in anguish, but the pain burned so intensely that she couldn't hear her own screams. Dropping the keys, her legs collapsed, and she fell to the ground. The woman did not let up, zealously sucking her blood.

Bridget gagged as she felt the blood drain out of her body. She tried to stab the woman, but the woman knocked the knife from her hand easily. She flailed her arms in pain as the vampire ripped her neck open, tearing at it like a candy bag and flinging the bloody flesh against the walls. Bridget grew faint as her oxygen was cut off. The woman shoved her whole mouth into Bridget's exposed windpipe, slurping and licking up every last stream of blood she could. Her tongue felt like sticky, rough sandpaper against the inside of Bridget's neck.

When the woman released her, Bridget's knees fell into a pool of her own blood gushing out beneath her. She saw her own flesh dangling before her and the woman with a blood-soaked face smiling at her.

"Worthy," the woman said in a darkly warm voice, blood dripping from her mouth.

Bridget collapsed lifelessly onto the floor.

The scream from Bridget was all the motivation Cate needed to toss caution to the fucking wind. She hastily tore open the closet door and sprinted out into the bedroom. She almost fumbled her bat but clutched it all the tighter, screaming blindly in fear at the dark night. Bursting from the bedroom, she dashed madly through the living room.

She barely registered the dark shape huddled over Bridget's now lifeless corpse, sucking blood from her open neck. Cate stumbled over something as she ran.

The keys!

Not worrying about how they got there, she snatched them up and bolted for the kitchen. She heard the dark shape hiss behind her, and the sudden wave of dread redirected itself at her.

She would have only moments—seconds—to get out the back door, start the car, and floor it out of there. There was no saving Bridget now. It was either Cate save herself or end up like Bridget.

You've lost another one, Cate.

Shattered glass crunched under her shoes as she ran through the kitchen, leaping over the bloodied crutches in the process. Throwing open the broken backdoor, she dashed down the wooden porch and turned left towards the driveway with the car. The first hints of dawn glowed dimly in the otherwise darkened sky. Desperate to make each second count, she fumbled with the keys.

There were five keys, and each one looked like a house key.

Which one? Which one? Cate thought frantically.

As she reached the car door, she tried the first one.

It didn't fit.

She tried another key.

It didn't fit either.

The wave of dread grew greater and greater. Those precious seconds turned into milliseconds.

The third key didn't fit. Desperate, Cate took her bat and smashed the driver's window in. Reaching inside and unlocking the door, she yanked open the door and started to climb into the driver's seat. Before she could get completely in, however, a powerful hand grabbed her by the hair and yanked her forcefully back onto the grass.

Falling on her back, she saw the woman in black now standing over her.

Whatever dread she'd felt being chased by the man at the gas station now seemed like a distant, pleasant memory compared to this. Blood dripped from the woman's face—*Bridget's blood!*—her fangs out and stained red. Her hood was off now revealing long, flowing dark hair that blew gently in the wind. More than anything, her face radiated pure hatred.

Before the vampire could attack, Cate rolled out of the way and stood back up, facing the woman. She raised her bat to swing but stopped.

The vampire stared her in the eyes, calm and collected.

Cate felt terror seize her spine. She froze in place, unable to will herself to move.

"Worthy," the woman said, smiling a malicious smirk while licking her lips. With fangs bared, the woman approached Cate.

I'm sorry Bridget. I'm sorry Sarah. Wherever you are, I'm so sorry.

The woman in black yanked Cate's neck into position and bit hard. Cate screamed as her neck burned. Everything soon went black.

Where am I? How long have I been here?

It was dark in this room, but the sky was beginning to light up a little. She felt the aura too, but it meant nothing to her now.

There was a pain in her stomach, but her neck felt strangely cold. Numb.

Her thoughts were disjointed and chaotic.

Who am I? What is this place?

Yet the place looked familiar to her. She knew she must know the place. She was hiding here. Looking for something.

Keys.

Keys to start something.

The car.

She saw blood caked on the floor.

My blood.

The pain in her stomach tightened. Burned.

So thirsty. So hungry. Can't remember when I ate last.

Standing up, she looked at the wall. It was splattered with blood.

I need blood. I need it. Who am I?

She reached up to feel her neck. The pain from before was gone. She expected to feel an open flap of skin, but to her surprise she felt the rough tracing of a scar. Her open neck had begun healing itself. She wiped away some of the blood and flung it from her fingers.

I need blood. I'm so hungry.

She heard movement behind her and turned around.

There stood the woman in black wiping her bloody mouth off with her cloak sleeve. The woman stared at her with a devilish smile.

"Feeling better, child?" the woman smirked.

Her. I remember her. She's the one who did this to me. I want to tear her to pieces.

She crouched instinctively like a tiger readying to pounce on the woman. Something told her that this wouldn't cure the gnawing pain in her stomach. But it would ease the anger she now felt.

I remember now. My name was Bridget. I am Bridget.

Bridget leaped at the woman, but the woman merely shoved her back. Bridget fell to the floor, her head smacking the side of the bookcase. It didn't hurt, though. Not really.

No. I was Bridget. I'm something more, now.

The woman glared at her. "I was a goddess long

before you were born, child," she hissed. "Your quarrel is not with me. The blood that you seek is scurrying west. Out there." The woman pointed towards the windows, but Bridget did not look. She eyed the woman with a venomous stare.

I will kill her. I must kill her.

They both heard a snarl from the dining room. The woman spun around. Standing there was another woman, covered in blood from the neck down. She looked familiar to Bridget.

I know her. She's a friend. Yes, a friend.

The other woman glared violently at the woman in black, also ready to pounce. With each passing second, Bridget's memories pieced themselves back together.

Yes. A friend. Cate.

The woman in black quickly turned back towards Bridget and stared her in the eyes. Bridget sensed the woman was trying to will her to freeze in place, but it wasn't working. The aura of dread was gone. Bridget's anger rendered it useless.

Bridget stood up and glared right back at the woman.

She read behind those glowing eyes a sad, dark history. She thought she sensed that they once were blue. This woman had built up a wall of rage to conceal several lifetimes of sorrow and loss. That rage might have terrified mere mortals, but Bridget understood the only truth that mattered anymore: *I am not mortal anymore. I'm just like you.*

"The foes you seek are out there!" the woman commanded, a hint of fear in her voice.

Fearing death no longer, Bridget pounced again, and Cate did likewise from the other side. They both grabbed the woman by her arms and started to pull. The woman let out a demonic howl that echoed throughout the house. As the woman tried to break free, they both stepped on her legs, pinning her in place. The woman frantically tried to catch their eyes, desperately willing them to stop and freeze in place. But her glare of rage revealed one of abject terror, a realization that her dark reign was about to continue without her.

As she pinned the woman and pulled on her right arm, Cate caught the fearful glimpse in the woman's eyes. It was like staring into the face of a ravenous, wild beast that knew it was about to die. She knew, as she was sure Bridget knew, that this woman would try to kill them if they let up. She pulled harder.

The arms began to rip apart. The woman lashed frantically, screaming. Black cloth tore, followed soon after by the sound of flesh and bone breaking off. With a final pull, they ripped both of her arms off. The woman in black screamed in pain as dark blood gushed out of both sockets.

Blood. Plenty of it. But I want more, Cate thought.

Cate and Bridget then grabbed her by the shoulders and forced her to the ground. The woman gnashed her teeth and snarled, but those teeth meant nothing to them as they began taking turns biting into her cheeks and skull and neck and torso. Their fangs ripped apart the woman's cold flesh. Each time they tore away at her skin, they raised their heads up and spat away her fleshy chunks to the carpet.

All at once, the woman stopped screaming and looked up, tears in her eyes.

"I am coming home, Darling," she rasped as something not unlike a desperate smile broke out on her face. To Cate, it didn't look like the face of someone afraid of death. It looked more like . . .

Joy? Relief?

The woman closed her eyes, smiling. Tears from underneath her eyelids ran and mixed with the bloody pool that gathered underneath them.

"You don't get to enjoy this," Bridget hissed.

Bridget pressed her powerful hands down on the woman's neck, crushing the woman's throat in. With a crunch, her neck finally caved in, and the woman's eyes bulged out. Whatever relief the woman thought she'd found was soon gone as they both started digging their fingers into her dark robe. Clawing through to her skin, they punctured her chest and tore it open, spraying blood everywhere. The woman, whose neck was crushed, let out a broken scream as they pried open her rib cage and tore apart the black and bloody innards that remained. Some of the bones snapped in the process, so Cate tossed them aside. There was a heart, two lungs, and the usual organs, but it had all been stained black and purple. A heavy pool of blood saturated the carpet beneath them, their knees soaking in it.

Blood. We will take your blood, Cate thought.

Together, they began pulling on the woman's head. Cate was really getting annoyed at that screaming. She sensed Bridget was too, who kept pulling more frantically each time the woman screamed.

The screaming stopped as they heard her neck snap and break apart. Twisting and pulling together, they ripped the woman's head off and threw it at the wall.

The woman in black's body twitched for several moments, then ceased. Blood ran freely across the floor as Cate and Bridget leaned down to drink their fill.

Sunlight began to pierce the sky now. Not a sound could be heard anywhere.

Then Cate stepped out onto the porch followed by Bridget. They descended the stairs together.

The woman had been more of a warm-up snack than a real meal. She wasn't fresh or pure like the humans would be. She was cold and clammy, like a rotted meal that offered no reprieve from the pain gnawing at their stomachs.

Once on the grass, Cate turned to look at her companion.

She is a friend. Yes, a friend. She's like me. Bridget.

Bridget looked at her and nodded.

Cate nodded back.

Together, they moved swiftly in what they thought was west, where they realized they'd have a better chance of satisfying this new hunger that burned within.

OCTOBER 31st

Lex had never felt so tired and delirious in all of her life. Her increasingly heavy eyelids made driving straight and fast difficult.

She still couldn't believe she'd found a red truck with the keys still in it. Even better, the tank was nearly full, so she'd make it not only out of Asheville, but maybe even a good ways west before having to fill up again. She didn't even mind that the name J-E-S-S-I-E was sprawled out in big white letters on the back window. She was just glad the thing worked, and she was finally getting out of there.

Why didn't I just leave? she kept asking herself, sweating and shivering at the same time. She already couldn't remember what had been so important. Memories of the past few weeks came back to her as fleeting images that were dulled and disconnected from any emotional attachment.

The disappearances on television.

The bunker Dana's family owned.

A few weeks hiding out with her sorority sisters and Dana's boyfriend's family.

The night a vampire got in.

The bloody carnage as she and Kari barely escaped into the night.

Lex still didn't know how the vampire had gotten in. The bunker door had been well hidden and locked tight with bolts and internal mechanisms like a bank's vault.

She didn't want to think about that night. She didn't want to think about Dana's neck being ripped open. She didn't want to think about Kassandra, one of her sorority sisters who'd just been turned into a vampire, pinning Dana's boyfriend to the ground and biting into his throat. She didn't want to remember that unsettling scream Kassandra made that didn't sound human.

That had been two days ago. Each night since she'd been trying to hide and escape west as much as possible, avoiding the vampires. One caught Kari almost immediately the next day. Lex just kept running, leaving her friend and past life far behind.

That morning, as she navigated the empty downtown streets, she found the red truck abandoned next to an alley. Its door was open. A trail of dark, dried blood led from the seat to the ground and across the street where it finally ended down a storm drain. The truck looked like a temporary hiding place at first, but when she saw the keys still in the ignition, she decided to get the hell out of there. Soda cans littered the truck's floor. She tiptoed quietly around these as she sat in the driver's seat and turned the keys.

In hindsight, it was probably the sound of the truck roaring to life that attracted the vampire to her.

It was a little kid about eight years old. She looked lost and helpless. Dirty. Hadn't slept. Dust and ash dyed the girl's curly, blonde hair. Her purple shirt looked ragged and caked with dark mud and crusty, dried blood. The stain partially obscured the picture of a horse. Something about the cautious way the girl moved made Lex think the girl was trying to hide from vampires herself.

Lex opened the door a little, her foot on the brake pedal, and motioned to the girl.

"You okay?" she said, loud enough for the girl to hear but quietly enough to not echo throughout the empty streets.

The girl stopped at the truck but didn't respond. She looked exhausted and didn't even seem to really notice Lex. Her thousand-yard stare communicated all the horrors she must have experienced.

Lex thought she could sympathize. Wanting to leave quickly but also wanting to help the girl, she tried to encourage her.

"Hey, I'm getting out of here. You want to come with me? My name's Lex. I'm a good person. We're gonna leave the vampires behind. We'll get somewhere safe out west. What's your name?"

The girl looked up and stared directly at Lex. Horror struck Lex as she saw the glowing white eyes of the child vampire.

"I am Daughter," the girl said calmly, and before Lex could move, the girl leaped with blinding agility and started biting at her neck. The girl was so tiny that Lex was able to shove her off fairly easily. Pushing the girl back out onto the street, Lex slammed the gas pedal down and took off. Going probably sixty through the downtown, she didn't look back to see if the girl was chasing her.

She just had to leave as fast as she could. Had to find an exit. Had to get west.

And now here she was, barreling down I-40 two hours later while rubbing that sore spot on her neck. She could feel the two, tiny puncture holes the girl left. They weren't bleeding much—the girl hadn't bitten very hard—and so they were already congealed over.

Lex reached into her mouth to feel her teeth. Her canines didn't feel any sharper. But she felt so delirious and tired now.

I'm going to turn into one of them.

As she continued down the road, she saw a group of people walking by the side of the road. There were about six or seven of them, all bundled with coats. As she got nearer, they turned to stare at her in unison. Even at this distance, she could see their eyes glowing white and their fangs dripping with the blood of whatever fresh kill they'd feasted on.

She floored the pedal and sped past them.

Just gotta go west.

In her rearview mirror, the group of people moved in what seemed like a kind of slow solidarity. Though she was faster, they were still moving westward after her.

ACKNOWLEDGEMENTS

This anthology grew out of an idea to explore a fictional vampire plague from various perspectives in the form of multiple short films. As time went on, it evolved into a collection of interconnected short stories told in prose. Getting from one version of this idea to its final form required a lot of help that I am deeply grateful for.

First, I want to thank Carlie Brooks, Kerstin VanHuss, Lori Franklin, Angie Gragg, and Tyler Brooks for helping me tell the first version of this story. Their involvement as cast and crew in the original short film *October '95* (2019) helped establish the basic concept and bring this alternate 1995 to life. I couldn't have done it without them.

Thank you to my wife, Anna, for patiently listening to all my bonkers ideas, hearing me read each story in painstaking detail, and then giving me the blunt and honest truth about what worked and what didn't. That's to say nothing of her incredible work on the cover art.

My beta readers spot problems and offer creative solutions that I often fail to catch. I am deeply grateful to each of them for taking time out of their lives to read my stories and give me invaluable feedback. A very special thank you goes out to Alivia Chapla, Carlie Brooks, and Katrina Makkouk.

Thanks to my brother, Andrew Bailey, who answered my questions and provided feedback on the technical, procedural, and biological aspects of being a paramedic and riding in an ambulance car.

I feel it's only right to give final thanks to Joseph Sheridan Le Fanu, who wrote the original vampire story that my tales draw their lore from. Without his original novella, *Carmilla*, there would be no Mother or her lost Beloved.

ABOUT THE AUTHOR

STEVEN BAILEY was born December 3, 1988 in Marietta, Georgia. He taught high school English for ten years before transitioning to focus on writing. He is the author of the novel *When Joni Died* and the creator of the short horror films *Nightmare of the Masked Lady* and *October '95*. He currently lives in North Carolina with his wife, Anna.